Sometimes being true to yourself means
sacrificing everything

———————————

Joel Espen could never be who he really was in the small
town of Haven. Still, there was always something different
about him. Sixteen years old. Green eyes that could see
right into your heart. A selfless need to save people. Even the
way he died reflected the way he lived: helping others. But
how are you supposed to just go on living like normal after
suddenly losing your brother… your best friend… your
first love?

As the six teens who were closest to Joel try to find the
meaning behind his death, they begin to realize that tragedy
can sometimes set you free—by revealing who you truly
are.

THE
WAY HE
LIVED

In loving memory of Madame Elaine Dubois,
and for all those who suffer in silence.

THE
WAY HE
LIVED

EMILY WING SMITH

Woodbury, Minnesota

First Edition
First Printing, 2008

Book design by Steffani Sawyer
Cover design by Gavin Dayton Duffy
Cover image © 2008 by Image Source/SuperStock

Flux, an imprint of Llewellyn Publications

Library of Congress Cataloging-in-Publication Data
Smith, Emily Wing, 1980–
  The way he lived / Emily Wing Smith.—1st ed.
    p. cm.
  ISBN 978-0-7387-1404-2
  1. Teenage boys—Death—Fiction. 2. Mormons—Fiction.
  3. Utah—Fiction. I. Title.
  PS3619.M584W39 2008
  813'.6—dc22
                  2008024416

Flux
Llewellyn Publications
A Division of Llewellyn Worldwide, Ltd.
2143 Wooddale Drive, Dept. 978-0-7387-1404-2
Woodbury, MN 55125-2989, U.S.A.
www.fluxnow.com

Printed in the United States of America

Acknowledgments

Many thanks to Margaret Bechard, without whom this book would not exist; to Janet Thorpe, for teaching me about so much (including Miss America); to Dad, who loves debate but loves me more—your help was invaluable; to everyone at Flux who shaped this story; to my advisors and friends at Vermont College, especially my beloved Whirligigs (Carrie Jones, I owe this all to you); to my peeps at Casa de Huiso—truly, you guys are awesome, I love you; to my writer posse Kim, Bree, Sara, and Valynne who offered insight, ideas, and hope; and to Daniel—for introducing me to Joel, then standing back and letting me get to know him.

Funeral Service for Joel Everett Espen

Invocation .... Todd Espen
Opening Hymn .... *Amazing Grace*
Eulogy .... Tabbatha Espen
Speaker .... Mark Espen, Jr.
Remarks .... President Brent Bedall
Closing Hymn .... *How Great Thou Art*
Benediction .... Lily Espen

Monday's child is fair of face
Tuesday's child is full of grace
Wednesday's child is full of woe
Thursday's child has far to go
Friday's child is loving and giving
Saturday's child must work hard for a living
But the child that's born on the Sabbath day
Is fair and wise and good and gay.

IN LOVING MEMORY
JUNE 24, 1990–JUNE 10, 2007

Pallbearers:
Todd Espen
Mark Espen, Jr.
Miles McGuire
Glenn Peterson
Lloyd M. Peterson
Paul Smith

Monday's child is fair of face.

AUGUST 10–SEPTEMBER 1

TABBATHA

Mood: worried   :-s
Music: Gnarls Barkley *Crazy*

I am worried because I have no idea how to write a blog.
I am crazy because I had a nervous breakdown last year.

Now I don't have anything left to write. My mood
and my music sum it all up.

So far this isn't a very interesting blog, I know.

My next entry will be better, though.

August 11

I guess I should have started by introducing myself, and
my blog.

I'm Tabbatha Espen. Eighteen years old. My inter-
ests include reading, doing crossword puzzles, and
eating chocolate. I just graduated from Haven High
School. My ACT score is 35. My SAT is 2270, com-
bined. I was going to go to Smith College this fall. Now
I don't know what I'm doing.

My family includes me, my mother and father, my
little sister Claire (15), and my late brother, Joel. I don't
know if you call someone your "late brother" if he died
when he was still a kid. Joel was almost 17 when he
died, so technically he wasn't a kid. He was an adoles-
cent. Anyway, that's my family.

You may be thinking, "Why is this girl keeping a blog? She sure isn't very good at it."

This is true.

Joel was the one who wanted me to start a blog. He said, "Tabs, you're a good writer. They have some cool sites where you can start a journal on the web. You know, where other people can see it. You should try it."

I didn't get the point of having a journal where everyone could see it; I still don't. But Joel wanted me to do it, so I'm doing it.

Fulfilling the wishes of a dead guy.

It is my neurotic way of handling it.

August 12
Mood: reflective   :-?
Music: The Beatles *The Long and Winding Road*

Gone.

It's been nine weeks since my brother died.

I wasn't there when it happened, but the people who were tell me that it was four o'clock in the afternoon when his eyes rolled into the back of his head and they knew he was gone.

So right now, at this very moment, it's been *exactly* nine weeks.

It's an interesting thing, being gone.

I mean, that's how I think of Joel since he died: that he's gone. But there are a lot of ways to be gone. Like this year, I was going to be gone. I was going to Smith College, which is Back East, as opposed to Out West, where I live. If I were gone, then like Joel I wouldn't be around for Sunday dinners or holiday weekends.

Nine weeks isn't even a whole semester. If I was gone for nine weeks, I don't think my mom would even miss me. Honestly, I'm not just saying that. I think I would come home for Christmas and she would say, "Tabbatha, it seems like you just left!" And the whole vacation she would be saying things like: "I bet you can't wait to get back to school, can you?"

But with Joel gone, she notices every day. We all notice Joel gone every day.

I notice other kinds of gone, and I wonder if anybody else does. Like Dad is gone. He goes into the office so early that sometimes I don't even see him before he leaves, and when he gets back I'm often already asleep. And speaking of being asleep: my mom is sleeping a lot more than she usually does. So in a way, she's gone, too.

Now there's another kind of gone. It happened today, which is Sunday, and the only day of the week everybody is home. Mom and Dad sat down with Claire and me right after church and told us that we're moving.

They've already closed on a house. Apparently "closed on" means case closed. They aren't asking us if we *can* move, they're telling us we *will* move. As in, they've already hired movers for Saturday.

This Saturday we're moving to Haven.

Haven is less than a mile from West Haven, where we live now, but it's in another world.

Outsiders don't know that the city of Haven is made up of two very distinct sections. It is, I believe, the last place on earth to have a proverbial "wrong side of the tracks." Everything west of the railroad tracks is drained out swampland where land is cheap and, according to Havenites, so are the people. We've had a three-bedroom, one-and-a-half bath bungalow (circa 1933) out here in West Haven since I was two years old.

We grew up here.

I'm not ready to be gone.

August 14
Mood: tired of packing |-[
Music: Joni Mitchell *Big Yellow Taxi*

I went crazy and started seeing a therapist way before Joel died and the rest of my family started needing a therapist. But they don't have a therapist. I do. Her name is Cathy.

It was 9:10 this morning when I got to the medical center where Cathy works, and the meteorologist on the waiting room television said it was nearing 91 degrees. I wished the temperature would reach 91 before the clock reached 9:20. If it stayed in the 9:10s and the temperature made it to 91, then the temperature would be 10 percent of the time. Puzzles like that fascinate me.

"How has this week been going?" Cathy asked me as we walked to her office. "How are the headaches?"

"Not so bad," I told her.

They aren't so bad. Not like they used to be back when things were expected of me.

The sunlight radiated through her office. Cathy loves the sun, probably more for its warmth than its light. I started seeing her on April 24, and she has worn a jacket at each of our sessions so far. Cathy sat on her usual chair, not saying anything. Probably waiting for me to say something.

"So," I said, stalling. "So, uh …"

I never know what to say to Cathy. What do you say to a shrink when your brother just died, but that's not why you're crazy?

Okay, this diversion is officially over. I went to Cathy's this morning. Now I'm packing.

Welcome to my world.

Same day, 2:30 p.m.

I just realized that maybe I should explain why I see Cathy. The thing I don't get about blogs is how much backstory to tell. I mean, a journal is easy. You don't need a backstory because it's your life, and unless you have a really bad memory (which I don't) you remember major events leading to other major events.

The major event that led to Cathy was this: All my

life I've been an "overachiever." You know that girl in the front of the class, with pale skin and glasses? The one who wrecks the curve and turns in extra-credit assignments early? The one who reads during recess and hopes it rains during PE? The one who goes to science camp in the summers? That was me.

People were always asking if the pressure got to me, and I was like, "What pressure?" Life was just life.

By senior year I had everything: 4.0 GPA, a billion AP credits, and an early acceptance to Smith.

Then, in the spring, when everything was supposed to be winding down and I was supposed to be slacking off and dreaming of college, the whole nervous break-down happened. I was always busy planning gradua-tion with the rest of the graduation committee, or at a final-exam study session, or a lunch meeting for some club or another. I forgot to eat, forgot how to sleep. Just felt . . . numb.

And then one day, I couldn't find my good diction-ary. Not the lame abridged version, but my real diction-ary—the hardcover I won in the school spelling bee. I don't know how long I had been looking for it—seri-ously, like *searching* for it—when Claire came in.

I was crying hysterically. Every drawer was upturned and swept out. I was reorganizing the closet. Why? Was I thinking I had accidentally shoved it in between my sweaters after looking up "millinery"? I don't know—I was in the middle of a psychotic episode at the time. And Claire was right there, watching it happen.

Do I even need to say she got freaked?

Not like I blame her. I was the big sister—helped her with homework, drove her places, took care of her when Mom was having an off-day and couldn't. I was the one in control.

Then, one day, I wasn't.

Claire talked to Mom and Dad, who talked to my doctor. He was the one who talked to Cathy.

August 16

I Always Helped Serve At Everybody Else's Funeral.

Whenever someone died I was there, whether it was an old spinster down the street or the father of four school-aged children whose heart gave out.

That's what I was thinking about during Joel's funeral. I had just given the eulogy—Mom wanted me to do it because I was a debater, good with public speaking and good with words.

It was easy to talk about Joel. You know how usually at funerals when people talk about how good the deceased was they're exaggerating? I didn't have to.

"Joel died the way he lived—helping others," I told everyone, even though they already knew.

I was dry-eyed and straight-faced for the whole thing, and as I turned to go back to my seat I wondered who was going to serve lunch. Whoever it was, I hoped they knew where the church tablecloths were stored, the ones that look all lacey but are really made out of plastic so they're easy to wipe down.

Uncle Mark was saying how sometimes we can't see the big picture, but God can.

Give me a break. How generic. He could have said that at a funeral for *anyone*. He was supposed to be talking about Joel.

I wondered if they would use centerpieces at the luncheon. Usually after funerals the church ladies cater a meal in the gym, and sometimes they decorate with these really putrid arrangements of dried flowers.

I hoped they wouldn't do that today.

Some high-ranking church guy was speaking. I didn't know him. He didn't know Joel. Listening to him didn't seem to have much point.

My mind kept coming back to the luncheon.

I could already taste what we would eat. Standard Mormon funeral fare: green Jell-O, potato casserole (the kind with cornflakes on top), chicken salad sandwiches on croissants. Cookies for dessert. That's the part I remembered most: serving cookies to the deceased's survivors.

Only this time the church ladies would be serving cookies to me.

Mood: angry   X-(
Music: Madonna *This Used to be My Playground*

Moving Day.
    I don't want to talk about it.

August 19
Mood: disgusted   :-u
Music: Hymn #274 *The Iron Rod*

I hate going to church here. I hate the Knob Farms 2nd Ward.

    I go to church with kids from the new neighborhood, of course—the golden boys and the so-totally-popular girls I knew at Haven High, back when I was just some genius-geek from the wrong side of the tracks. Now I'm in Haven, and I can tell by how everyone looks at me out the sides of their eyes that they wonder about me. Not just the going-crazy part, either, or the dead-brother part, but the how'd-a-family-from-West-Haven-afford-a-house-*here* part.

    I'm sure everyone thinks it's some kind of mystery, like we had a huge life insurance policy on Joel (we didn't) or we sold all our earthly possessions (we didn't) or we went on church welfare to afford a bigger house (do I even need to say we didn't?).

    The truth isn't so interesting: Dad had stock options

in his company, and when it got bought by a bigger company about five years ago, we got rich. We paid off the West Haven house, put Joel in gymnastics, sent me to debate camp and Claire to regular camp. Sometimes I don't think Claire even remembers being poor, eating spaghetti with canned tomato sauce and knock-off Cheerios from a bag.

I do.

That makes it hurt worse, living here.

It's like we've left everything behind.

Same day, 5:32 p.m.

My mother said she hoped my stay at home would be like living in a "sanitorium."

She really said that.

Back then, my "stay at home" was in the house I'd grown up in with a family who loved me. Now I live with my sister who's scared of me, my dad who's barely home, my mother who's jealous of me, and the memory of my dead brother. In a seven-bedroom, four-and-a-half-bath "sanitorium."

With a pool.

I was scared to tell her I wasn't going to go to Smith this fall; that I was deferring admission. But I knew the deferring admission part would soften the blow: I had one year to get better, no more. That's what I'm doing this year. "Recovering," as Cathy says. I was afraid that when I told my mom about the decision, she'd lose it.

But she didn't. She said she was jealous. She said it so quickly I knew it was the first emotion she felt: jealousy. Not fear. Not concern. Jealousy.

I thought her first emotion would be embarrassment. I mean it's embarrassing to have your brilliant, accomplished daughter defer her college enrollment so she can stay home and "recover" from her psychosis. Isn't it? It definitely gives people a negative impression of our family. And for as long as I can remember, Mom has been telling us to make sure we "give people a good impression of our family."

Which was why I couldn't believe the poem she put on Joel's funeral program. Joel's favorite poem was this nursery rhyme he'd learned when he was five and memorized *The Complete Mother Goose* in its entirety. Joel always had a good memory, just like me. Anyway, you know that one about a different child born on each day of the week? Joel loved that. So it makes sense that it'd be sort of like, you know, an epitaph for him. Except that the last line of the poem goes, "the child born on the Sabbath day is fair and wise and good and gay." Yeah. Because it was *Mother Goose*, and written way before our time. Joel was born on a Sunday. So you figure it out. How does implying that your dead son was gay (*not* the case) give people a good impression of your family?

I don't know. I guess what other people thought of

our family wasn't what she was thinking about, the same way it wasn't what she was thinking about when I told her I wasn't going to Smith. Right then, she was thinking that now I got to stay in a sanitorium and she wanted to stay in one, too. Maybe a brief stay in a sanitorium would have helped her combat her off-days. She's had those ever since I was little. And it made perfect sense to me. She wanted a break, too. After all, *she* never got let off the hook from living life because she was crazy.

At the time, I decided I would rather have her feel envious of my illness and treatment than I would have her be repulsed by it.

But today I'm thinking maybe that's why we're here now. In this house that feels nothing like our old house, like our home. We are in this place where we get up and go to bed and pretend to function. But really, Mom, and Dad, and me, and maybe Claire although I wouldn't know—we have all been let off the hook from living life.

And we're doing a bang-up job.

Haven is a narrow city, and from our new house, which is its highest point, I can see all of it. Out the back window I watch the sunset over the lake, brilliant shades of auburn-gold.

It reminds me of a book I read, about a girl who was crazy like me, only she was locked up for real. The chapter-heading read: "Every Window on Alcatraz has a View of San Francisco."

That's how I feel now: like I'm staring into a city that isn't entirely normal, but from a place that is much stranger.

August 20

I guess other blogs have links to other websites and articles and quizzes and stuff. If you are perusing my blog hoping to find such items, I recommend stopping here. There is nothing like that in this blog. There are no places to post comments. Honestly, I can't imagine why anyone would want total strangers (or worse, total acquaintances) to respond to their innermost thoughts. I don't want to know what anybody thinks about crazy me, or my crazy family.

I especially don't want to know what anybody thinks about Joel.

I just want to write it all down. If I were writing it for me I'd keep all this stuff to myself, but I'm writing it for Joel. Not that I really believe Joel is in some heavenly Internet café, checking out the blogosphere. But still.

I'm not doing it for you. I'm not doing it for me.

I'm doing it for Joel.

I've reconsidered.

It took me awhile, but I reconsidered.

I'm posting an article. Even though I don't want to. I think Joel would want me to. I think Joel would say, "Tabs, tell them what happened. They need to know. But more importantly, you need to tell them."

And I know why he would say that.

It's because every time I think about how he died, I start to scream.

Not loud, blood-curdling screams. Almost more like oversized moans than screams. But every time I remember the policeman coming to the door or the reporters coming to the house or any bit of finding out that he was gone, I don't start to cry. I start to yell.

Repeatedly.

I know this can't be healthy.

For the last few months, I've been swallowing lava when I remember how Joel died.

I doubt letting you read one of the articles is going to make me stop.

But it might help.

Scout Dies in Grand Canyon, No Water to Blame

BY JONAH THOMPSON, STAFF WRITER

WEST HAVEN—It was three days into their hike in Grand Canyon National Park when Joel Espen's Boy Scout group ran out of water.

Long after the three adult leaders of the group had succumbed to the 112-degree heat, Espen, 16, and Miles McGuire, 17, were rushing to the Colorado River to get water.

Only Espen never made it to the river. He collapsed from heat exhaustion and dehydration a few hundred yards away.

"Joel kept urging everyone on to the river," said Samantha Matheson, whose son Cade was one of the hikers. "My son told me Joel gave all he had to help others, including his water."

The group consisted of Scoutmaster Paul Smith, brothers and Scouting veterans Lloyd and Glenn Peterson, and five boys. The hikers couldn't have been more prepared and equipped, Smith emphasized. "The boys knew the area and so did the leaders ... [Espen's death] was nobody's fault. It was a combination of factors that couldn't be helped."

Still, the boy's death raises questions about the preparations of the group, whose trip was authorized by the Boy Scout Council. Each hiker carried approximately two gallons of water, deemed adequate by Smith, the only hiker to have traveled the route before. But according to Grand Canyon National Park spokeswoman Denise Jacobs, more than twice that much is recommended for a three-day hike, especially in direct sunlight.

After the group ran out of water, Smith was the first to be disabled by the heat. He hid under the shade of a rock while the others continued toward the river. Shortly after that, the other two adults on the trip also needed refuge and sought shade. This left the boys on their own.

"Of all of them, Joel should have made it," said Smith. "He was the toughest one of all."

August 21

A Day in the Life of Tabbatha M. Espen:

5:15: Rise. This is a habit I've had since junior high, one that I've found impossible to break even now when there is no earthly reason to get up this early. Go upstairs into the "breakfast nook" to read the paper and make hot chocolate. Longingly remember the days of an eat-in kitchen. Throw a breakfast pastry into the toaster. Breakfast pastries are one of the few benefits I see to being rich. These are a far cry from your generic Pop-Tart breakfast. These pastries come with squeeze-it-yourself icing. How cool is that?

Roughly 6:00: Say goodbye to Dad, who is headed to work (I figured out what time he usually leaves each morning so I can be there to see him off. Which is good, since I won't see him again until late this evening, if at all). He kisses me on the head, but doesn't say anything.

Sometime between 7:10 and 7:15: Go to the gym to begin cardio workout. (I've been going to the gym almost every day post-breakdown. Cathy says getting my physical health back on track will help my mental health get back on track, too. Maybe she's right.)

8:00: Shower, get dressed, and check in on Mom, who is usually still sleeping.

Day Activities:

- Reading (right now I'm in the middle of a biography of Oprah). Each day I can generally read one nonfiction book, one "classic," and sometimes one of the novels on the New York Times Best-Seller List, too.

- Writing in my blog   :-)

- Appointments
- Cathy on Tuesday
- Phil, my personal trainer, on Monday and Wednesday
- Doctor appointments on Friday:
    1. dermatologist ("to cure the havoc stress has wreaked on your skin" says Mom) OR
    2. dietician (to make sure I remember to eat: "no repeats of the 'breakdown'—that's the last thing this family needs") OR
    3. usual physician ("so we don't underestimate the link between mind and body")

Please note: all these are "standing appointments." Ah, you've never heard of such a thing, you say? Well, it means that long ago, before Joel died, back when my mother was still envious of my broken-down, emotionally fragile state in the sanitorium, she made appointments with Cathy et al. and said basically, "meet weekly (or however often) until further notice." I have obviously not been cured yet, because the standing appointments still stand.

Evenings: Dad is still at work. Mom is usually watching TV in her room or reading. Occasionally she wanders into the kitchen, remembering we should have dinner. But that's rare. Usually Claire and I make frozen dinners or order something on the credit card Mom gave me. Sometimes I try to make small talk, but it never works. Claire's afraid of me.

Same day, later
Mood: confused   :-z
Music: Handel's *Messiah*

Have you ever had a day when you feel like you're living in some surreal, parallel universe where everything is not only opposite of everything you thought you knew, but so ironically twisted it makes you question whether or not you ever knew *anything*?

I've been having those days all the time lately.

Today I went to see Cathy. Which isn't strange, since I see her every Tuesday. And today she gave me a homework assignment, which also isn't strange. She gives me a homework assignment every week. I'm very good at homework. Cathy says that this will help me "get *more* out of therapy." Which is definitely good, because I personally have never understood why you have to go to school for years to learn how to *give* therapy, but you don't have to go to school at all to learn how to *get* therapy.

I mean, at our sessions, I work just as hard as Cathy does. I tell her about the things she asks me to tell her about, I visualize the things she tells me to visualize. I work hard. Only I haven't been trained. I don't know if I'm doing it right.

But homework?

That I can do.

Anyway, this week's homework assignment is to talk to one new person each day. I know—lame. But talking to people isn't really my strong point. I mean, I can talk *at* them—e.g., debate team, college interview, presentation in English class—but talking *to* them is another story. So talking to one new person a day is a reasonable goal, but still a stretch.

So, I was washing my hands after our session, in the big restroom near the center of the medical complex, the one all patients can use whether they're going to get foot surgery or an eye exam or whatever. The strange thing is this: standing next to me at the sink, re-applying her already-plenty-heavy burgundy lipstick, was a women, in her fifties maybe, wearing black slacks, black heels, and a rhinestone-studded jacket. From her ears dangled huge rhinestone earrings shaped like tear drops. On a Tuesday morning.

Which brings me to another question: have you ever said something and immediately regretted it? Not later that night, when you're lying in bed, still awake because you realize that earlier that day you said something you regret. But *immediately* after you say it? Have you immediately wanted to vanish, or start over, or say you have a rare form of Tourette's or something?

That's what happened when I talked to this lady,

who was dressed like she was going to the Oscars on a Tuesday morning. I asked what seemed logical to me:

"Are you going someplace?" I motioned to her outfit.

I was proud of myself for already fulfilling my homework for the day. It meant I could just stay home for the rest of the day and didn't have to make up some stupid errand so I could find someone to talk to.

I'm very good at homework.

But then I realized something. And I asked myself: "Why did you ask her if she's going someplace? She's *obviously* going someplace! Probably she's getting chemo this afternoon and she wants to look her best! You are an idiot for bringing this up, and for reminding her that she has what is most likely a terminal form of cancer!"

Wow. I'm exhausted, the same way I'm exhausted when I finish a session with Cathy, so I'm signing off for now. But this is a good story, once you get over the stupid-crazy-Tabs part.

So I'll finish it later. Promise.

Same day, even later

Okay. I'm better now. Took some time off. Did some deep breathing.

Where was I?

Ah, yes. I asked the well-dressed woman in the restroom where she was going.

And she told me she was going to pageant rehearsal. Then she gave me a long look—an embarrassingly long, thorough look from head to toe—and said (this is verbatim): "Are you involved with pageants, dear?"

"Pageants?" I was thinking of the Christmas pageant at church. I played Mary two years in a row.

But somehow I didn't think that was quite what she meant.

I was fairly sure I knew what she meant. Beauty pageants.

The thing is, I'm not the beauty pageant type. For starters, you have to be beautiful to be "involved with pageants." Correct me if I'm wrong, readers, but isn't that the point? Didn't they recently take the talent portion out of the Miss America contest or something like that? Because it's about being beautiful?

I'm not some ultra-feminist pageant-hater. If people want to be "involved with pageants," they can go right ahead. But do I look like that person?

The answer is no. Here is the person I am: the Smart One. I have been the Smart One since I learned to read at four years old. And Mom, Dad, Grandma, et al. would call me variations on the Smart One ("one smart cookie," "a sharp kid," etc). Which was fine with me. I liked being the Smart One. Mom would always introduce me as "Tabbatha, the smart one," and it made me so happy to please her like that.

Besides, we were all something. Claire was the Baby, the Cutie. Joel was the Nice Guy. It was just who we were.

I was never the Pretty One. I'm not pretty. Not like I'm saying "boo-hoo, I'm not pretty." I'm just not. I've always known that.

Anyway, I was just standing there, thinking about not being pretty, when she said: "Pageants. You know. *Scholarship competitions.*"

So, just to make sure we were on the same page, and that she was indeed crazier than I am, I said: "Like Miss America?"

Again, this is verbatim because, as I told you, I have an excellent memory: "Oh, you don't start with Miss America, dear," she said, brushing something invisible from my cheek. I flinched, but not before I noticed her enormous rhinestone ring. "There's a local contest first, usually at the city level, or the county. Have you ever done anything like that?"

What could I say? Except: "No."

So she said, while rummaging around in a gigantic black purse: "Well, then take my card."

And she was gone, leaving me to stare at her card, which read:

Destiny Fairchild
Consultant to the STARS!

My question to you, dear readers, is this: Is Destiny Fairchild her *real* name?

August 22

Mood: thoughtful   :-?
Music: Switchfoot *I Dare You to Move*

Joel called me Farrah Face.

He was the only one who did.

It was because of that poem he memorized—the one about each child born on a different day of the week.

I was Monday's Child.

"You're Farrah face," Joel said one night. Mom was reading *Mother Goose*—again. "Tabbatha's Farrah-faced!"

"Fair *of* face." I corrected him just as I usually did, being the older sister. "Not Farrah face."

If you knew my mother's sister, Aunt Farrah, you'd know she had a face no child would envy. She wore foundation about six shades too light for her skin. It made her look like one of the scary clowns in the circus. Her eyelids were a freakish powder blue, and her lashes stuck together like they were coated with molasses.

"Farrah face," he said again, chuckling.

"Fair *of* face," I said again, louder. "Fair of face!" I was yelling.

"Tabbatha, shh," Mom said. I wanted her to defend me. I thought she would. But instead she just said, "shh."

"Make him stop calling me Farrah face! Make him tell me I'm fair of face!"

"Oh, give it up, Tabbatha." Mom sighed. Under her breath: "Farrah face is more accurate, anyway."

Do you think she didn't think I heard her? Or that I didn't understand? That I was too young to realize I was the Smart One, not the Pretty One? Well I did: hear her, I mean, and understand.

So that night I was crying myself to sleep in the room I shared with Claire. My mother, wouldn't you think she knew why I was crying? But she never apologized for hurting me.

Joel did.

"Don't cry, Tabs," he said, and he was out of his room and next to my bed. "I think you're fair of face."

Even back then he wasn't like other little brothers.

August 23

I confess: I checked out Destiny Fairchild's website.

How could I not? It was calling out to me like I was Pandora.

There's a lot more to this pageant stuff than Vaseline and duct tape.

But it's still one crazy box.

Advice from Destiny:

- For photo shoots, pick a simple outfit. You can never go wrong with simplicity.
- Your hair is your crowning glory.

- Keep your face visible from all angles.
- Remember, hair can make or break your appearance.
- Body makeup is a must for the swimsuit competition.
- Jewelry should be kept to a minimum (pearls are recommended).
- Your evening gown is the most important outfit you will wear in front of the judges, the media, and the audience.
- Success will meet those who go confidently in the direction of their dreams

Click here to check it out for yourself.

August 24
Mood: invigorated   :-§
Music: Anything and everything *School House Rock*

Technically, all of Destiny's advice was from Destiny.

But Destiny wasn't the first one to say that last thing, about going confidently in the direction of your dreams. It was actually Thoreau.

She could probably get in trouble for using his words without giving him credit, but the truth is, it was actually a pretty bad paraphrase anyway. Because I just read *Walden*. And the real quote is: "If one advances confidently in the direction of his dreams, and endeavors to live the life which he has imagined, he will meet with a success unexpected in common hours."

I know. *Way* better, right?

So I thought about my dreams—the life I had imagined.

Before the craziness, before Joel was gone, back when I really *felt* things, I had dreams. Most of them were goals, goals that I knew the Smart One should have. Get into a great college. Get into a great Master's program. Get my PhD somewhere so fantastic that I could become a professor at the school of my choosing. Smart things. Those were my dreams.

I don't know about my dreams now. For a while, I didn't have any. It was like dreaming took up too much energy. All I could do was get up and get dressed and go to the doctor and read a book and go to sleep and after I did all that, there was none of me left.

But I want to dream again. I want to write more.

It could be because I've been keeping this blog, and realizing it's not as hard as I thought it was going to be. Or it could be because of Destiny Fairchild, telling me I could become one of her STARS. I don't know.

I've decided to take a writing class.

I enrolled at the University—thanks to rolling admissions and my being such an "ideal candidate" they accepted me even though school starts just a few days from now. It's three credits, ones that will probably transfer to Smith. Not that I know I'm going to Smith. Not that I know I'm going anywhere, for real.

All I know is that the U is close enough that I can drive there on Mondays, Wednesdays, and Fridays and it won't interfere with my appointments. Plus, it's only one class—nothing too stressful. Nothing to push me over the edge.

Joel would want me to do it.

I start Monday at nine.

Same day, later.

I called Cathy, and she likes the idea.

So does Mom. In fact, when I talked to her about it, she gave me her full attention. And she never gives anyone (or anything) her full attention. She said it sounded "great." Her eyes got brighter, and I was sure she was going to ask to see the course catalog or take me back-to-school-shopping.

But she didn't. She said: "You can use the credit card to pay tuition."

Typical. But better than nothing.

August 26

I love the first day of school.

I've always loved the first day of school, ever since I started kindergarten. There is just nothing like it: freshly sharpened pencils with erasers so clean and untouched you don't want to make a mistake, notebooks without midterm battle scars, highlighters that still work.

I love all of it.

August 27

Class was pretty basic today.

Our professor, Margaret "Call-Me-Maggie" Beuchart-Hale, is someone who obviously thinks highly of herself because she's published in various literary magazines that nobody's heard of. Still, I like her. She has long, wild red hair and she's nice. Before I would have thought: "She's a teacher. She's supposed to be smart. Who cares if she's nice?" Things like being nice matter to me more now, though. I guess that's one of the things you learn when you go crazy.

She wanted to get to know us and our writing style, so she said to write something for Wednesday that "moves us deeply."

You know what?

I'm going to write about Joel.

Something that Moves Me Deeply: JOEL

So, my dear readers, today was my first real day of class. Although I didn't post it on my blog, I actually did write my assignment. It was more about leaving our house after Joel died than it was about Joel, though.

I was in my room writing about Joel, and even though I tried not to I started wanting to scream, and then I really was screaming. Much louder than I usually do. Much longer than I usually do, too.

And nobody noticed. Granted, Dad was still at work. Maybe Claire had the TV turned up. My room is downstairs and Mom's isn't. But still. Shouldn't someone have heard? Shouldn't someone have come into my room and said: "Tabs, are you okay?"

I stopped screaming, and all I could hear was my computer humming—and *not another sound*. Like I was in a haunted house where you hear screaming, then silence. So I thought about that. How our new house is kind of like a haunted house. Maybe haunted by Joel—not that he's a ghost, or that he ever lived here. But maybe he's wondering what's going on with his family, the one that used to at least "give people a good impression."

I wrote about that, and I didn't feel like screaming anymore, and I finished the piece.

Now, readers, I want to tell you this *exactly the way it happened* because this classroom episode is perhaps as bizarre, or more so, than the whole Destiny Fairchild incident. Go with me now to my writing class, this morning.

Maggie puts us into groups to read our pieces aloud so we can get to know each other. Personally, I think this is a scary way to get to know people—by sharing Something that Moves Us Deeply with them. That could just be me, though. I *am* the girl who had to be assigned to talk to people, after all.

There are five in my group: one guy I swear I went to high school with named Todd; an intense-looking blond girl with an infected nose-piercing named Angeline; a middle-aged man named Doug who I can tell I'm going to hate by the way he mispronounces "inevitable" (I hate it when people use words they don't know how to say); a tall, well-dressed guy who looks Pakistani or Persian or something named Alexander; and me.

Todd wants to go last. Angeline has written a minimalist poem about berries, which move her in some way I have yet to determine. Doug has written an exposé on his supposed affair with his secretary. Alexander looks over at me. I can tell he's seriously doubting that this guy even *has* a secretary. I smile just a little bit. Alexander is thinking like me. Nobody thinks like me. At least, I thought nobody thinks like me. So already I'm feeling better than I have in quite a while.

We comment on these pieces like we're supposed to, with noncommittal murmurs and Angeline and Doug trying to out-do each other by using obscure literary terms.

I like what Alexander's written. He writes about the different schools he went to growing up: how he started in Sweden and finally ended up in the U.S., even though his father is Middle Eastern and his mother is French.

Then it's my turn.

When I read I'm not expecting a problem, since I switched my subject from one that made me start screaming to one that I had more control over. Besides, I was debate club captain in high school—I'm a good public speaker and I'm good with words. I'm the Smart One.

So it's stupid, but by the time I finish reading I'm literally choking up. I don't want to cry—the last time I cried was the time I couldn't find my good dictionary. I can do this without crying. I can finish this. And I do.

There's only a few seconds that go by after I finish reading and then Doug says: "Impossible. I mean, just the logistics of it. There's no way your parents could move so quickly after their son died."

I am about to punch Doug right square in the nose. I have never punched another person before, and I bet it will break my hand because I've seen that in movies.

It hurts to punch someone when you don't know how to punch. But I do not care.

I want to yell at him. I want to say: "How do you know? Have you ever *tried* to move so quickly after someone in your family died? I have, and it sucks, but it's possible—unlike you ever getting it on with anyone you don't have to pay, you bastard."

I hope that since this is the Internet, no one is offended by the language in this entry. Needless to say, this is not the kind of language I usually use. But this is the kind of language that comes to mind when you are about to punch someone right square in the nose.

Luckily for both Doug and me, Alexander clears his throat and says, before I can do anything: "I think Tabbatha's story sounds too real for me to get hung up on little details like dates. Besides, I've moved in that short a time before. Sometimes the fact that you have to move that quickly is more significant than the move itself." He has a calm, soothing voice with a European accent I can't place, but it sounds right on him.

I've cooled down enough that I don't want to punch Doug anymore, and I don't even care when Angeline starts talking about a book she once read with a situation just like this one.

I smile at Alexander. He smiles back at me.

I've made a friend.

After class I talk to Alexander. I want to talk to Alexander, and I probably would have even without practicing Cathy's homework assignment all last week. So I tell him how much I appreciate his defending me in front of Doug. I am also thinking how usually I have trouble talking to guys, but with Alexander it's totally natural.

Anyway, Alexander smiles and says: "You looked ready to kill him. I don't blame you. He's a total shit-head."

I'm surprised to hear someone say that who's as calm and collected and nice as Alexander. Most of the nice people I know don't swear, but Alexander is totally nice. He says he liked my piece (!) and I say I liked his, too.

It is hard for me to explain in writing what happens next. It sounds weird and almost rude in writing, but it really wasn't. It was wonderful. He looks at my face very closely and says: "You should let me pluck your eyebrows."

I've always wanted to pluck my eyebrows. They have grown in thick and bushy since I was about nine. Think Bert on *Sesame Street*. Every time I try to pluck them, I have a sneezing fit so severe I can't even hold the tweezers, let alone pluck in the right place. Once I tried waxing them: I ended up with fat eyebrows about a half an inch long. "Hey, Groucho," said Joel when he saw me. "Fair of face," I reminded him, and that shut him up.

So it's no small thing, offering to pluck my eyebrows. To make sure he realizes this, I say: "You'd really pluck my eyebrows for me?"

Alexander nods. "I pluck my own eyebrows all the time."

I wonder if he's studying cosmetology. But if so, why is he taking a writing class? Then I start yelling at myself (in my head, don't worry) because I'm stereotyping him! Like an uneducated person would do! He can take writing classes AND cosmetology classes. He's a well-rounded human being!

While I am berating myself, Alexander is clapping his hands and saying: "We could do a whole makeover!"

This is a mannerism just begging for a stereotype, but perhaps it is not what it looks like. Perhaps this boy who plucks his eyebrows and offered to give me a makeover and is easy for me to talk to ... maybe he isn't gay.

But sometimes stereotypes are stereotypes for a reason—because they're accurate.

I don't have time to ponder this because I am thinking: a makeover entails me going to his house, or him coming to my house, and I can't remember the last time I've gone to someone's house, and I've *never* had someone over to my new house, and on one hand I don't want him to come over to my new house, which he knows is possibly haunted, but on the other hand I can't go to his house because I don't go *anywhere* unless it's school or church or the gym or a medical center. So thoughts are swirling in my head that have nothing to do with his sexual orientation.

Anyway, the only thing I can think to say is: "I don't have very much makeup." Which is true, but is still a stupid response.

But he doesn't notice, I don't think, because he just tells me to bring what I have, and can I come over on Saturday, and is three o' clock okay? And I nod, because I can't say anything, I can't even believe this is happening, because just recently I only talked to people as an assignment and now I am going over to hang out with a friend like a *normal person*. He asks me where I live, and I say Haven, and I am about to explain where it is but he says that *he lives in Haven, too*!

I don't mean to wrinkle my nose or sound so surprised, but I must because Alexander laughs at me when I say: "You do?" He says: "Why does that shock you?"

And it shocks me because in Haven a guy who goes around offering to pluck a girl's eyebrows is either making fun of someone for being gay or asking to get beat up. Alexander and Haven bring up two images in my mind that I can't force together. It's like imagining the Teletubbies in Communist Russia.

Anyway, he gives me his address—a condo right across from Fitzgerald Market—and says he'll see me on Saturday.

Seriously, guys, this is big: I've made a friend.

I'm writing this late Saturday night, and everything has changed.

I want you guys to experience what happened today the way I experienced what happened today. Not that I necessarily think anyone's reading this. But just in case someone is, I want you to feel exactly what I felt.

Saturday afternoon I am so excited to go to Alexander's house. Excitement: like little ginger-ale bubbles bursting in my stomach.

His condo is *nice*—and not just the way that everything in Haven is nice, either. It's in a brand-new complex with stucco and stone and columns. It's way too nice for a college kid.

A guy with spiky yellow hair answers the door.

The ginger-ale bubbles in my stomach go flat. I've got the wrong house. I finally get invited to someone's place and I go to the WRONG ONE. I'm trying to think of what to say when the yellow-haired (not blond) kid says: "Hi. I'm Ian. You must be Tabbatha—Alexander's told me all about you. Come on in."

He smiles, and just like that—no more panic. I step inside.

On the walls are paintings—honest-to-goodness

paintings—and there's other swanky stuff all over the place: leather couches, a flat-screen TV.

I can tell immediately that Ian is gay. It's not just the way he talks—in that stereotyped gay way, complete with hand gestures—or his excellent taste. It is the way he complains about his hands being dry and proceeds to rub them with cherry-vanilla lotion—and then offers me some.

He's gay, and he's not afraid to let people know it. I would be. I bet everyone I know would be.

Alexander comes down the stairs with a blow-dryer and a makeup kit in hand and a Fitzgerald's Market grocery sack around his arm.

I can't believe Alexander, my sweet, exotic Alexander, shops at Fitzgerald's Market just like all my new neighbors.

"Look what I've got!" he calls out, and starts unloading things onto the counter. He holds out a box of hair dye. It looks blackish purple. I'm thinking: He's changing my hair? And also: Do I want purple hair?

"It's just for underneath," he says. "Lowlights because your hair's so thick."

How comforting?

Anyway, then Alexander is telling me that I'll need to change my shirt before we work on my hair. He thinks maybe Adam has something I can borrow.

I ask the obvious: "Who's Adam?"

"Our housemate," says Ian. "His clothes are hideous. We'd be doing him a favor to destroy one of his shirts with dye."

"His room's down the hall on the left. You go borrow something while we finish setting up," says Alexander.

He wants me to go into a stranger's room and borrow a shirt? Is he crazy?

Then I remember: I'm the one who's in therapy. I'm the one who's had a breakdown. How do I know what—or who—is crazy? As I walk down the hall and turn left, I wonder if Adam's gay. Until a few days ago, I didn't think anybody who was gay would live in Haven. Maybe if you're like Ian and possibly Alexander and don't care who hates you, you can be gay in Haven. But what about regular people? People who care what other people think of them?

I hear soft alternative-rock playing. I knock on the door.

ADAM: "It's open."

He doesn't ask who it is. I would have preferred that, but I go in anyway. Adam is sitting on his bed in near darkness, strumming on his guitar. His bed is unmade and doesn't have any blankets on it. There's a faded Roger Rabbit sheet hanging over the window instead of a curtain. Clothes are everywhere. He's still in what I think are his pajamas: gray sweats and a black polo. And I think he's trying to grow a goatee or something, because his chin looks extra stubbly. Not like I'm that familiar with stubble, but still. Yuck.

ADAM: Hi.

ME: Hi. I'm Tabbatha. Alexander's friend.

ADAM: Nice to meet you.

ME: (trying to sound natural) Alexander and Ian thought maybe I could borrow a T-shirt from you. Would that be okay?

ADAM: (starts strumming again, softly, but loud enough to irritate me—I'm TALKING to him, and the least he could do is pay attention) You look fine to me.

(It occurs to me that Adam is likely not gay.)

ME: I know I look fine. I need to look unfine while we dye my hair.

ADAM: (still playing) And that's why you came to me? To make you look unfine?

ME: (forcing politeness, the kind I used with other kids when I was in high school and had to talk to people) May I please borrow a beat-up T-shirt to wear while my hair is being colored?

ADAM: (gets up and wiggles open his stuck middle drawer that's missing a knob) What's your problem?

ME: *My* problem?

ADAM: Yeah, your problem. (Throws a shirt at me and I manage to catch it. I smooth it out and read the lettering on the front: *With Liberty and Justice for All.* Then, in smaller letters: *Some restrictions apply. Void where prohibited.*)

ME: (ready to leave) Thank you.

ADAM: I didn't mean it in a bad way.

ME: You didn't mean to ask me what my problem is in a bad way?

ADAM: (setting the guitar back in its case, like a peace offering) What I meant ... you just look like you have a problem. You look ... I don't know. Like you've been worried for a long time.

ME: So?

ADAM: Yeah, I get it. You don't know me from Adam. (Smiles, although this joke is very lame even to me, a girl who enjoys the occasional lame joke.) But seriously. I want to know why you're so worried.

ME: Why?

ADAM: (shrugging) Why not?

Why not? It's true. My life is out here on my blog for all you guys to read—if anyone, in fact, is reading this. And I already wrote and read about it in front of people like Doug and Angeline. I don't have any secrets. I don't want any secrets. Keeping them isn't worth the energy.

ME: I'm crazy. And my brother died. My mother wasn't there for us to begin with and now she's gone farther away. My dad's gone, too. He's never around. We moved to this rich snobby neighborhood that Joel would have hated. That's my brother. Joel.

ADAM: The one who died?

ME: (nods)

ADAM: How do you know Joel would hate it? Did he tell you?

ME: Oh, no. I'm not *that* crazy. Joel doesn't talk to me. He didn't have to tell me he would hate how everybody's handling him being gone. I just know.

ADAM: You don't seem crazy at all to me.

ME: You don't know me that well.

ADAM: I know you well enough to know you aren't crazy.

ME: If you really knew me you wouldn't say that.

ADAM: Listen to me. (Pauses to make sure I'm listening. Not like those people who say: "Listen to this!" but don't care if you're actually listening or not.) You aren't crazy. I know crazy. And you aren't it.

The thing is that I believe him. I don't know him, or anything about him, but I trust him. Maybe it's because of Destiny and because I signed up for a class and talked about Joel without screaming. Maybe it's because I'm feeling strong and I've actually gone to a friend's house and now I'm having a conversation with a total stranger and don't feel even the slightest bit like I'm shrinking inside myself. Or maybe it really is that I trust him. But I believe him when he says I'm not crazy.

I've gotten so used to my craziness being part of me, though, that it's too weird to think of myself without it.

ME: Thanks for the shirt.

ADAM: Thanks for telling me.

Who's gay? Who's crazy? Who knows?

Who cares?

I come back to the kitchen to see Alexander mixing something up in a container and Ian tearing squares of aluminum foil from a long roll. Did you know people use actual aluminum foil when they're doing hair?

"Perfect! We're ready for you here. Come sit down next to the sink," Alexander says. I obey.

Ian looks at me. "I'd kill for a waxing kit," he says.

Alexander sighs. "Yeah, these are … more intense than I thought." He looks at me. "Close your eyes."

I do, so I only see darkness. Except it's not some scary, evil darkness. It's like the darkness makes me feel things ten times stronger: Alexander's fingers, strong and soothing, as he washes my hair. The peppermint shampoo with tea tree oil tingling my scalp. My eyes are closed, but I'm feeling things, *seeing* things more than ever before.

The thing is, guys, that I stopped looking at myself a long time ago.

I don't know when, but once I figured out that I was smart and not pretty, I didn't look at myself anymore. I would get up and go to the mirror and make sure I didn't have sleep in my eyes and that my hair was combed or braided, whatever it took to make my appearance scholarly. But I didn't see what I looked like. I didn't see myself as anything other than the Smart One. I didn't need to look at myself to know that. You hear about some people, "looks are all they have"—I always pitied those people. But the thing I didn't realize was that I was one of those people, too. Except instead of looks, all I had were smarts.

Then, after the breakdown, when Mom looked at me and I could tell I wasn't her Smart One anymore, I felt like I didn't have anything left.

Because if I wasn't the Smart One, who was I?

"You look like a supermodel," Ian said.

I thought about going home and showing Mom my supermodel-self. It made me smile. It makes me smile now, too.

"No," Alexander said, "she looks like Miss America."

And I smiled again, because hey, it wouldn't be the craziest thing to happen to me this year.

Tuesday's child is full of grace.

SEPTEMBER 7

ADLEN

Adlen Murray is riding in the passenger seat of her dad's Toyota Avalon on Friday morning: tournament day. She always rides to school with her dad. He drops her off on his way to work at a law firm downtown.

Technically, Adlen could drive herself to school. She has a license and a car. But she shares the car with her brother K.L., who takes it to early morning football practice.

Football is K.L.'s thing. Debate is Adlen's thing.

"You nervous?" asks Dad, turning down the AC.

It's a rhetorical question. She's always nervous before a debate tournament. Today after school is her first tournament of the season, and she doesn't even have a partner. Not a real partner, at least.

"You can carry her," Dad says, referring to Heather, Adlen's unreal partner. "Just make sure she's got the basics down. All she has to do is be competent." He turns the AC off.

Honestly, Adlen probably can carry Heather—not literally, of course. Literally, she'll be carrying the giant Rubbermaid tub full of debate evidence that weighs down her every step.

Last year, the tub currently in the Avalon's trunk belonged to Tabbatha Espen, who neatly printed her name across the lid in black Sharpie. Debaters are a strange breed, chronicling history in their own unique way. Each year, the debate club captain uses this particular box, labeling it with his or her name. Tabbatha was last year's debate club captain, and even then it was obvious that Adlen would be the box's next owner.

Adlen looks at her dad. She never used to look at him—she already knew what she'd see: a big guy with dark hair and glasses. Adlen has always been close to her dad, and it was never what he looked like that mattered. But last year, when she started debating, she started really looking at him.

Dad loves debate. She'd always known he was a natural, having heard his stories about his days in high school and college debate, having seen the trophies and the pictures. But she hadn't *known* it: the way his eyes got alive when he talked with her about a new case, or the way he smiled his real smile when discussing the tournament with her later. Adlen knows her dad. She knows he has a real smile, one he hardly ever uses, and a fake smile, the one he uses the rest of the time—when a situation warrants a smile but he doesn't find it particularly pleasant or amusing.

Adlen has a real smile and a fake smile, too. Adlen is a natural debater, too. She watches her dad.

"Make sure she's competent," he is saying. "You be the one to shine."

He is smiling his real smile.

Dad drops her off at the side of the school, at the entrance near the debate classroom. He pops the trunk. "Need help bringing it in?'

Adlen pictures herself walking into Haven High

with her father beside her—dressed in a dark suit and carrying a green Rubbermaid tub, like a bodyguard who thinks he's a professional mover.

"No, I can get it," she says.

Dad nods. "Have a great day, Adlen. I wish I could be at the tournament with you."

"Heather's driving," Adlen reminds him. Heather volunteered to drive, less than crazy about the idea of Adlen's dad taking them.

"Yeah, I know. Call me if you need anything, though?"

"I will." Adlen hops out of the car, both her backpack straps already across her shoulders. "Love you."

"Love you, too," Dad says, as Adlen lifts the green tub out of the Avalon's trunk.

On the way to the debate classroom, as she wrestles to hold the tub, Adlen is queasy. Thoughts of debate are the only ones that make her queasy. It is 7:15 a.m. Approximately nine hours in which to dread the tournament. Nine hours to figure out how not to lose.

When Adlen first started debating last year, she told Dad about the queasiness. He said it would go away once she got used to tournament days.

She's been to eleven tournaments since then.

Her organs still feel like they're tipping over inside her abdomen.

As she goes up the stairs, Adlen's mind gets queasy

as well. It's a new sensation for her. Thoughts tip over in her brain like the organs in her stomach.

She imagines the dizziness coming from free-floating individual facts, personified as murmuring little green men. Her head is like the bounce house her elementary school inflated for Field Day every year. The green men jump and bounce, their murmuring becoming an unbearable buzzing.

All she can think about is getting them to calm down—to fit together like pieces of a jigsaw puzzle. She likes puzzles, likes making sense of things, likes her thoughts linking together naturally. She likes facts that help her solve puzzles, not facts that jump and bounce and are of no use whatsoever.

The door to the debate room is open, and Adlen drops the tub in the corner of the room. The tub contains all the evidence she and Heather will use at the tournament today, and since it's too big to fit in her locker, she stores it here. Tami, an orator, and Nikki, who does student congress, are talking to the debate coach, Mr. Wills. Usually they would talk to Adlen, too, but they know enough to avoid her on tournament days.

She checks her watch: six minutes before school starts. Okay. She has a few minutes now and whatever time she can grab during first period to create a crash-course document to review with Heather during second period debate class. Adlen sits at the same desk she sits at during debate class and exhales slowly. This never helps her relieve stress, even though it supposedly works for everybody else. She keeps trying, thinking someday it will work for her, too. Apparently today is not that day.

She digs her notebook out of her backpack and sees that it is already opened to a fresh page, as though anticipating her time constraint. Perfect. She'll write it all down. She'll make it all make sense.

Adlen Murray's first debate tournament of the season ("the tournament") begins in approximately nine hours. Keeping her from tournament victory is her new debate partner ("Heather"). Adlen must remedy Heather or face inevitable slaughter at the tournament. Consider:

1. The status quo won't make Heather better. Heather believes she is already good. Heather reports in 2007:

    Really, I don't get what the big deal is. We present a case. We tell the judge we're right. We tell the other team we're right. I already know how to win an argument, Addie; I'm always right.

    Furthermore, Heather's dad insists in '07:

    Heather's a natural debater. She loves to argue. She's been arguing with her brothers and sisters since she was knee-high to a grasshopper. Practice? A girl like Heather doesn't have to practice being angry.

2. It is up to Adlen to teach Heather debate skills before the tournament. Debate coach Arthur Wills in '07:

> *Frankly, Adlen, I don't even know much about debate. I came to this school with the intention of advising the newspaper staff [...] but it was either coach the debate team or the color guard. You seem to have this stuff pretty well down, since you were on the team last year. You can show Heather the ropes, right? You're a capable, intelligent girl.*

Plan: Adlen will give Heather a debate crash-course, entitled *What Heather Must Know*, during debate class. Instead of using this period for catching up on gossip/sleep, Heather must listen to everything Adlen has to say. With Heather's mild competence and Adlen's skill, the two will be saved from utter annihilation, and Adlen will again excel at debate, her thing.

The bell rings, signaling five minutes until class starts. Adlen's pleased with what she's written, though, and when she stands up the green men have stopped jumping and their murmuring has dulled almost enough for her to ignore it completely.

First period is released time.

Released time is what seminary is called at Haven High. In other parts of the world, Mormon high schoolers meet at someone's home before school to learn about scripture and get some spiritual perspective on their day. At Haven it's part of the school day. Students are "released" to the seminary building, which is just far enough away to be off school grounds but so close to campus that it backs onto the D-Zone of the parking lot.

Adlen hates released time.

This is interesting, since she's actually quite spiritual. Not spiritual in the Haven High School sense, which means if one is spiritual one is close to God, and thus inherently better than one who is not spiritual. Adlen is spiritual in what she believes is the truest sense of the word: she is spiritual the same way Dad is a debater, or K.L. is an athlete. The way a runner needs to run, the way a singer needs to sing—that is the way she feels close to the Spirit of God. It's how she finds strength.

But seminary doesn't give her that strength. Seminary lessons don't prick her heart like certain passages of the Book of Mormon or certain sacrament hymns do. More often than not, seminary makes her angry because it has so little to do with the divine. Maybe it is the debater in her that constantly wants to ask: what is the *point* of all this?

Especially today, when it is taking her away from what she needs to do: figure out how to win the tournament. Figure out how to do her thing, how to best use her gift. Figure out how to shine.

Adlen swings back the glass double doors. The seminary building is lighter than the school, and cleaner. The walls are decorated with pictures of Christ instead of reminders about yearbook photos and dance team tryouts. Outside the door to her classroom, she gets ambushed.

"Hi, Adlen!"

It's Beth. Beth is a senior and on the seminary council. It means she likes to know everybody's name and what everybody's into so she can "reach out." Adlen would rather not be reached, though—especially when it comes to well-meaning Seminary Council members.

"Hi, Beth." She forces a smile, showing just enough teeth.

"How are things with the debate club?"

Things with the debate club. Adlen considers telling Beth about things with the debate club. That the first tournament of the season starts today after school. That she's the team's only varsity debater. That her partner, Heather Hilton, just started debating this year, so she's had all of two week's practice. That she's pretty sure Heather only joined the team because she thought doing so might get her closer to Adlen's football-hunk big brother. That the "debate team," such as it is, is doomed.

But Beth doesn't want to know any of this. She just wants to ask. Her ability to reach out to others is one of the things that makes her spiritual.

So Adlen says: "Things are great. We have a competition today. Wish me luck?"

Beth smiles and crosses her fingers. "Oh, I know you'll be great! Will you give our opening prayer this morning?"

"I'd love to," Adlen says, again giving her fake smile. She puts her hand on the doorknob and Beth takes the hint.

"Thanks! You're the best!" Beth says, backing up. "Really!"

In seminary, they're supposed to be studying the Old Testament.

How Time Is Spent in Seminary:

- Time spent studying the Old Testament: 28%.
- Time spent starting class, singing hymn, saying prayer, reciting scripture, and hearing spiritual thought: 16%.
- Time devoted to sharing uninspiring personal experiences and random tangents: 56%.
- Time Adlen has to pay attention: >1%, when she says the prayer.

So Adlen says the prayer, takes out her scriptures, and takes out her notebook, already open to a clean, lined page.

To accomplish the proposed plan, Adlen presents the following crash-course:

What Heather Must Know:

1. Heather must not think she is smarter than Adlen. Adlen has been debating for over a year. Adlen attended an intensive six-week debate camp at Stanford over the summer. Heather lay by the pool reading *CosmoGirl!* over the summer.

2. Heather must read the evidence when she responds to an argument. She cannot just tell the other team that they're wrong. Refusing to read the evidence will result in a losing ballot.

3. Heather must understand their affirmative plan. If she doesn't understand the plan, she won't be able to give a convincing argument for why the U.S. should adopt it. Adlen knows the Plan and will answer any questions Heather has about the Plan.

4. Heather must know counter-plan theory. The other team will likely run a counter-plan against them, and Heather needs to attack it correctly, or the other team will win.

5. Heather must learn about topicality arguments. As Adlen's dad, debate guru, always says—

"So suicide is worse than murder?"

This is not what Adlen's dad, debate guru, always says. This is what some kid in Adlen's seminary class says.

Suicide is worse than murder?

Adlen looks down at her Bible, opened to Exodus. True, she hasn't exactly been following along. But she's pretty sure this isn't doctrine. The teacher, a thirtyish guy named Brother Monson, doesn't answer. He calls on another kid Adlen doesn't know. This one says: "Didn't one of the prophets say suicide is the most selfish thing you can do?"

"Sometimes people are so deep in the throes of sin that their judgment gets clouded," Brother Monson says. He tosses a dry-erase marker in the air. Catches it, one-handed. "They don't see any other way out. But that way out is repentance."

There are more things Heather Must Know, but Adlen can't focus. She questions Brother Monson's use of the phrase "throes of sin," but more than that she questions his whole response.

Adlen believes in repentance. She believes Jesus Christ provides a way to be free of sin. But how does that relate to suicide? Does the rest of the class actually believe people only kill themselves if they feel guilty, burdened by wrong choices? Adlen is baffled by this conclusion, like she is with a lot of what she's termed "seminary logic."

To keep from saying something and to keep from listening she turns back to the notebook, but when she tries to write she can still hear Brother Monson's voice knocking around her skull with the green men, and they're all laughing at her. It makes her mad—too mad to write, too mad to think.

So she starts drawing. A girl. The girl, she realizes, looks kind of like Beth. Not much like Beth, but enough that Adlen smiles her real smile. She draws a mud puddle around the girl, which turns into quicksand, which turns into a whirlwind. Then she adds a bubble coming out of her mouth: "Help! I'm caught in the throes of sin!"

The green men giggle at that, but they don't line up yet the way Adlen wants them to, so she finishes her list.

5. Heather must learn about topicality arguments. As Adlen's dad, debate guru, always says, topicality is the RFD debaters most often overlook. Heather must know that RFD is debate shorthand for "reason for decision"—the reason judges decide to vote for teams. Or against them. Judges cannot vote against Adlen and Heather. Debate is Adlen's thing.

Second period is debate.

Adlen takes her seat in the nearly empty classroom. Debate is a small class, anyway—surprise, surprise—but kids are often late because Mr. Wills lets the class get away with pretty much anything they want, since he is a new teacher and doesn't know better. Adlen is always on time.

In the corner of the room is her evidence tub, waiting patiently. The tub doesn't know how bad Heather is. The tub only knows how good Adlen is, and how good Joel was. Joel had been a great debate partner. Not because he was a great debater—debate wasn't even his thing—but because he'd known how not to screw up.

Tami and Nikki wander in and tell Mr. Wills, who's playing FreeCell on his computer, that the other kids (likely including Heather) have gone on a donut run. Typical debate class behavior on a Friday. Besides, it's tournament day only for Adlen and Heather. Everyone else goes to "individual event" tournaments. Dad says individual events are for chumps.

Heather is better suited for an individual event.

If you do an individual event, maybe an oratory, or a nice dramatic interpretation, it's okay to slack off. It's okay to go to Krispy Kreme instead of class. But Heather has not chosen an individual event. Heather has chosen to be debate partners with Adlen, so she is not allowed to be weighing the merits of cake v. glazed when she needs to be learning how not to lose.

While it may be true that Adlen's a control freak, it can't be said that she doesn't know how the debate team works. Mr. Wills' laissez-faire conduct is permissible, if annoying. But Heather? Heather's behavior is not allowed. Usually she is confrontational only during debate rounds, but Adlen makes an exception because right now she is just out-of-control enough to give Heather a piece of her mind.

Adlen imagines what her dad would do if he were in this position. Dad would make sure their evidence is organized and ready. She opens the box, double-checking each file. Dad would do speed drills. She times herself reading topicality frontlines, and clocks in at fifty-six seconds, beating her previous record of one minute two seconds.

Heather is still not there.

If it wasn't tournament day, and she was actually able to focus, Adlen would cut evidence for the new disadvantage she and her dad have been working on. But it *is* tournament day, and all Adlen feels are the bouncy green men turning somersaults in her head. She needs Heather to walk in the door. She needs Heather to sit down and listen.

As if in answer to her prayers, Matt Churchill, debate treasurer and slacker extraordinaire, waltzes into the classroom with two red and white donut boxes. Behind him are Dan, Kandis, and Ryan.

Adlen waits for others to shuffle in. Matt has been known to cram over a dozen seniors into his Highlander, and the entire debate class is not yet accounted for.

Jack and Lisa, their hands grazing, follow behind. Adlen waits; realizes she is holding her breath.

No Heather.

Heather to Adlen in '07, via personal communication (Post-It on Adlen's locker):

Addie!
Sorry I couldn't make it to debate class this morning—slept in! Meet me by the flagpole at lunch to discuss tournament? Thanks!

Point of Reference:

Last year, Joel Espen was Adlen's debate partner. He called her Nelda. He was the only one who did.

Adlen was named for her grandmother. Grandma doesn't care that her namesake isn't named Nelda, as that is such a hideous name that even Grandma goes by her middle name, Ann.

She doesn't tell people this, and generally people don't ask about her name, anyway. But Joel did. He asked her at their first tournament together, as they were setting up for the round. He had big, sincere eyes when he asked it, and he stopped getting out file folders and flow pads and really looked at her.

Nobody really looks at Adlen. They really look at K.L., because he is the tall, handsome one. He is the one with charisma. But Joel really looked at Adlen and said: "Where did you get the name 'Adlen'?" She was going to answer "from my parents" so he would feel stupid and lay off—except that he was looking and really seeing her. So she told him. "It's Nelda spelled backwards."

"Nelda," he said slowly, admiring the sound. "I'm going to call you that."

No one had ever given Adlen a nickname before.

No one even shortened her name. She felt close to him, then—close enough to tell him things she'd never told anyone. How much she hated debate. How it felt like a part of her, a God-given part, but she still wanted to change it. How she wanted to quit the debate team the way those born-beautiful brunettes sometimes still want to dye their hair blond.

She wanted to tell someone that she didn't like using her gift for debate, even though it was from God. She wanted to know if that meant she was denying the Spirit, denying that spark of divinity inside her. She thought Joel might listen. She thought Joel might understand. But when she tried to speak, she couldn't come up with the words.

Now Adlen's debate partner is Heather, who calls her Addie.

Third period is American history with Mrs. Andrew, and Adlen spends this American history period, as she does all the others, copying notes from the whiteboard while Mrs. Andrew works on the novel she's been writing ever since she started teaching at Haven ten years ago. Some people's idea of teaching is pathetic, but copying notes is just tedious enough to keep Adlen's mind occupied; her green men stay frozen in place.

After third period is lunch. Adlen sits on a cement bench beneath the flagpole, waiting for Heather and reviewing the crash course. Then revising it. They just won't have time to get through everything.

What Heather Must Know:

1. ~~Heather must not think she is smarter than Adlen. Adlen has been debating for over a year. Adlen attended an intensive six-week debate camp at Stanford over the summer. Heather lay by the pool reading *CosmoGirl!* over the summer.~~

2. Heather must read the evidence when she responds to an argument. She cannot just tell the other team that they're wrong. Refusing to read the evidence will result in a losing ballot.

3. Heather must understand their affirmative plan. If she doesn't understand the plan, she won't be able to give a convincing argument for why the U.S. should adopt it. Adlen knows the Plan and will answer any questions Heather has about the Plan.

4. Heather must know counter-plan theory. The other team will likely run a counter-plan against them, and Heather needs to attack it correctly, or the other team will win.

5. Heather must learn about topicality arguments. As Adlen's dad, debate guru, always says, topicality is the RFD debaters most often

overlook. Heather must know that RFD is debate shorthand for "reason for decision"— the reason judges decide to vote for teams. Or against them. Judges cannot vote against Adlen and Heather. Debate is Adlen's thing.

No Heather.

Adlen reads through the document until the words start to blur between her eyes. Absentmindedly, she flips to the next page in the notebook and starts drawing the school marquee.

The marquee is new this year, installed over the summer as a gift from the alumni association. Most of the Haven High alums still live in Haven, still want their school to look its best. Adlen sketches out the block letters—Haven High, Home of the Huskies—and the smaller, removable ones that spell out a message welcoming everyone back to school. Then she draws the husky itself.

The husky is named Harry. Haven's mascot. Adlen doesn't like dogs, but she tries to like Harry. As she draws, she relies on the rules of logic and symmetry— the ones she can no longer apply to the crash course. She sketches Harry's pointy ears and semi-protruding tongue.

"Hey, nice yeti!"

Yeti?

Adlen has not seen or heard Heather approaching

her. However, now Heather stands over her, looking at the marquee drawing.

"That's a yeti, right?" Heather points to Adlen's representation of Harry.

Adlen does not know Heather well enough yet to tell if this is an insult, a joke, or actual cluelessness.

From the way Heather acts in class, Adlen guesses it's the latter, but she still searches Heather's face for a trace of emotion. Finding none, she says: "Okay, I wanted to go over some stuff with you. First, I know what I'm doing, Heather." Adlen scoots over on the bench, making room for Heather to sit.

Heather stands. "Oh, I *know* you do, Addie," she says in a soothing voice that serves only to infuriate Adlen. "You love debate. I get that. But you don't have to worry about me. I'll be fine."

Adlen cringes at Heather's words: not just *I'll be fine*, but *you love debate*. She breathes deeply and says: "You'll be fine with just a little bit of training—"

Heather laughs, and the sound of it falls somewhere between harsh teasing and mild jeering. "Training? This isn't my first day on the job at McDonald's. Listen, I'll pick you up over there." She points to the pick-up/drop-off zone. "Give me any 'training'"—she makes the quote-marks with her fingers, annoying Adlen further—"on the way to the tournament, okay?"

"The ride's just a few minutes long—"

The bell rings. Lunch is over, and Adlen hasn't even

tried to eat anything. She can never eat on tournament days. Not before the tournament. Not during the tournament. Once the tournament is over, then she eats.

"Listen, I've got to run," says Heather. "Class is about to start."

This would be a reasonable excuse except that Adlen and Heather are going to the same class, Civics with Mr. Wills, and Heather is always late. Still, Heather is walking away, yelling, "Don't worry, everything will be fine" in her slightly nasal, totally irritating voice.

Everything is not going to be fine. Heather left without asking a single question about the tournament. She's never been to one, and she's not even *curious* about how they're run? She doesn't even *wonder* if Adlen brought their gigantic tub to school? She doesn't understand how serious this is. And she called Adlen's husky a yeti.

Adlen knows she is not a good artist. She has been told so many times, in so many words.

Miss Wallace in '98:

> *Don't worry about your drawing, Adlen. You have so many other talents!*

K.L. in '01:

> *Hey, I did the impossible—found a school subject Adlen actually isn't good at. Mr. Hess checked "above average" on every box on the report card*

except art! What kind of dork gets their lowest grade in art?

Dad in '03:

Trust me, Adlen, when you're a partner in some big firm in Washington, no one's going to care that your junior high art teacher said you couldn't draw a straight line. And you'll have the last laugh, because that art teacher? You'll be making ten times as much as him.

But a yeti?

She sees K.L. exiting the school on his way to the seminary building. He either doesn't see her, or does but is too busy to wave. Adlen assumes that all the football players must have exactly the same schedule, because K.L. is with four or five guys she recognizes from the team. There are also a bunch of nondescript shiny-haired girls around, but when aren't there? K.L. tosses a football in the air. Catches it, one-handed.

Adlen won her first debate trophy the same night that K.L. told the family he was probably going to be captain of the football team the next year. They were eating dinner. "Coach says I'm a natural," K.L. said before swallowing a forkful of mashed potatoes.

Dad was beaming. "That's terrific, K.L. Terrific! You are a natural. And Adlen, she's a natural, too. She won top speaker today, and this was only her second tournament."

Adlen knew she should love her brother, and usually she did. But she hated him at that moment, the same way she hates him now.

She hates him because he gets to love his God-given gift.

Fourth period is Civics.

Adlen is the only junior in Civics, because the class is usually reserved for seniors. Mr. Wills, who is also the debate coach, asked Adlen to enroll because given her debate skills, he thought she'd be a great candidate. Her dad acted like the invitation was the biggest honor in the world, but Adlen thinks it's more likely she was invited because Civics is notorious for its boredom factor, and Wills wanted to pump some life into the class.

Occasionally, Mr. Wills tries to liven things up by starting controversial discussions, but Adlen groans when she sees today's topic on the board. Resolved: the state constitution should be amended to define marriage as a union between only one man and one woman.

Wills is always bringing up homosexuality, trying to "open the students' minds."

It is one of the most pointless things you can do at a school like Haven, where "seminary logic" reigns supreme. And this topic. No one's going to be against it. Adlen's chest tightens again.

Tanner in '07:

I'll never say fags can get married. It's against my religion and you can't make me say it.

Jill in '07:

What kind of precedent would it set? That any freak could marry any other freak? We'll have people marrying trees and donkeys if we keep up with that mindset.

Heather in '07:

It's a tricky topic, Mr. Wills. In such a religious area.

"People still vote in religious areas, Heather," Mr. Wills says. Adlen knows what Mr. Wills is after. He's always trying to get kids to separate church and state. And every time, he thinks he'll have a breakthrough.

Adlen thinks it's more likely that one of these times he's going to get fired.

Mr. Wills looks at Adlen, silently begging her to say something.

"People may vote," Adlen says, "but they'll all vote the same way." She knows this. The last time the proposed amendment was on the ballot, it passed 92/8 in the Haven/West Haven area.

"It's because the people here know gay marriage is

wrong," says Heather. "They know being gay, period, is wrong."

"They *believe* gay marriage is wrong," Adlen says, looking her debate partner in the face. She hopes there's no hostility in her expression, but she knows that if there is, she can't do anything about it. "They *believe* being gay, period, is wrong."

"Same thing," says Heather.

Adlen doesn't even have the energy to get angry at this completely ludicrous argument. Besides, she knows that in this town, at this school, Heather is right. She looks at Mr. Wills and shrugs. It is the shrug of the resigned, the beaten.

Mr. Wills looks profoundly sad. Like on one level he is sad that yet another of his assignments has bombed. But on a deeper level he realizes that he won't be able to teach these kids anything they aren't willing to learn.

Adlen knows the feeling. She glances at Heather, who is high-fiving Tanner and looking smug.

This whole debate partner thing, Adlen thinks, is not going to work out.

What Heather Must Know:

1. ~~Heather must not think she is smarter than Adlen. Adlen has been debating for over a year. Adlen attended an intensive six-week debate camp at Stanford over the summer.~~

~~Heather lay by the pool reading *CosmoGirl!*
over the summer.~~

2. ~~Heather must read the evidence when she
responds to an argument. She cannot just
tell the other team that they're wrong. Refusing to read the evidence will result in a losing ballot.~~

3. Heather must understand their affirmative
plan. If she doesn't understand the plan, she
won't be able to give a convincing argument
for why the U.S. should adopt it. Adlen
knows the Plan and will answer any questions Heather has about the Plan.

4. Heather must know counter-plan theory.
The other team will likely run a counter-plan
against them, and Heather needs to attack it
correctly, or the other team will win.

5. Heather must learn about topicality arguments. As Adlen's dad, debate guru, always
says, topicality is the RFD debaters most
often overlook. Heather must know that
RFD is debate shorthand for "reason for decision"—the reason judges decide to vote for
teams. Or against them. Judges cannot vote
against Adlen and Heather. Debate is Adlen's
thing.

After school, Adlen waits in the pick-up/drop-off

zone. She is sitting on the lawn, the green tub at her feet, looking at her crash course/marquee drawing. She wants to pace. She thinks better when she is pacing. But you can't pace in the pick-up/drop-off zone. Pacing makes you look too eager. Code of conduct states that you sit on the lawn and look bored. So she is sitting as she waits for Heather, wishing she could pace.

There is the thud of a backpack hitting the ground next to her.

It's Joel's little sister. Claire. Adlen remembers her from the funeral.

Everything in her mind stops when she sees Claire. All she can think about is the look on Claire's face. She looks upset, but thoughtful. Lonely, but secure. Vulnerable, but defiant.

Trying to describe Claire is just another case in which Adlen can't come up with the words. A case in which critical thinking, keen observation—everything she's been blessed with—utterly fails her. A case in which her first impulse is to do something the complete opposite of her gift.

Adlen can't imagine what it must feel like to have your brother die—to be sitting on the same grass he was probably sitting on a year before, everything the same but everything unalterably changed. K.L. may be a natural at being a natural and she may be envious sometimes, but she still can feel the emptiness she knows would be there if K.L. weren't. She tries to imagine how she'd feel, losing her brother like Claire did.

She knows that's ridiculous. She heard that Joel died because he gave away the last of his water when his Boy Scout troop was hiking the Grand Canyon. K.L. would never give away the last of his water. Not because he's selfish, although he is. Because he would know he needed water to live. K.L.'s a jock, but he is capable of at least this much mental calculation.

Joel was capable of it, too, but for whatever reason he gave his water away and died of dehydration, and now Claire is sitting there, brotherless.

Adlen's fingers itch. She needs to draw Claire.

She shouldn't need it. She knows what she should need. For example, she should need to call Dad for advice. In fact, she should just ask Dad to come to the tournament and intimidate Heather into cooperation. But these needs are nowhere near as pressing as the simple need to take her pencil from behind her ear and capture Claire's exact expression.

First she works on Claire's face: her furrowed eyebrows, her straight-line mouth. Occasionally, she checks for Heather's car so that Claire won't feel her staring.

Claire looks like Joel: small, thin, pale skin with freckles. Adlen tries to put just enough Joel in her. Not too much, though. That's not all she is. Adlen draws Claire's jeans that are fraying at the bottom and her white athletic shoes that are graying. She draws the strawberry-blond braid hanging down Claire's back.

This time when she draws, it's different. This time, Adlen draws Claire the way she feels her. She doesn't funnel her ideas of logic and symmetry into her picture. She doesn't think about the curve of the line or the way one shape builds on the last one. She just draws, and it doesn't relax her. It does the opposite of relax her—only it does it in a good way. It pricks her heart, like certain passages from the Book of Mormon or certain sacrament hymns. It gives her strength.

And the drawing looks like Claire. It is the first portrait Adlen has drawn where the person is actually recognizable. Someone could pick up this picture and think hey, this is Joel's little sister.

Adlen hears a car horn honking like a too-loud alarm clock. It's not an attention-getting honk, it's an impatient honk, and she knows without looking that it's from a red Prius.

The green men start fidgeting. Her strength evaporates. Adlen flips the book closed, so she can forget about the drawing and concentrate on the highly-revised crash course. She'll just stuff it all away.

The notebook is blue.

Blue wouldn't matter, except that all Adlen's notebooks are yellow. K.L.'s notebooks are blue. It's been that way for every school year she can remember.

Dad. He must have seen the notebook lying around and, figuring only one of his children actually *used* a notebook, put it in Adlen's bag. Dad is so supportive of her. Especially when he gets to choose what to support her in.

There's a honk again, immediately followed by a loud: "Hurry up, Addie!"

There's no time to rip out the marquee drawing/crash course. There's only time to get up and grab the evidence box, wearing her backpack on both shoulders and holding the notebook between her teeth.

What Heather Must Know:

1. ~~Heather must not think she is smarter than Adlen. Adlen has been debating for over a year. Adlen attended an intensive six-week debate camp at Stanford over the summer. Heather lay by the pool reading *CosmoGirl!* over the summer.~~

2. ~~Heather must read the evidence when she responds to an argument. She cannot just tell the other team that they're wrong. Refusing to read the evidence will result in a losing ballot.~~

3. ~~Heather must understand their affirmative plan. If she doesn't understand the plan, she won't be able to give a convincing argument for why the U.S. should adopt it. Adlen~~

~~knows the Plan and will answer any ques-~~
~~tions Heather has about the Plan.~~

4. Heather must know counter-plan theory. The other team will likely run a counter-plan against them, and Heather needs to attack it correctly, or the other team will win.

5. Heather must learn about topicality arguments. As Adlen's dad, debate guru, always says, topicality is the RFD debaters most often overlook. Heather must know that RFD is debate shorthand for "reason for decision"— the reason judges decide to vote for teams. Or against them. Judges cannot vote against Adlen and Heather. Debate is Adlen's thing.

Sky Crest High School looks like a mall. There are bright lights and wide hallways, high ceilings and kiosks selling food. Instead of shopping bags, kids tote around boxes of evidence personalized by bumper stickers: *Stop the War, Free Tibet, UC Berkeley Debate.*

"I'm going to get a slice of pizza before we get started," says Heather. "You want one?"

"No thanks," Adlen says. "I'll check to see if postings are up."

The postings for the round are on the cafeteria doors. Heather and Adlen are up against Sky Crest's A-team this round: the best team from one of the better debate schools. Adlen tries to control her breathing. She can never breathe during debate tournaments.

She checks the pizza cart. No Heather. Adlen's gaze falls on the commons area, where Heather is flirting with some guy, holding her slice of pepperoni more like an accessory than a source of nourishment.

This is serious. This is important. They are going to be crushed at the one thing Adlen's good at and Heather's not even eating her stupid pizza.

Adlen's breathing is getting shallower, and the pain behind her eyes is back, and she can't read the map that will tell her how to get to room C105. She wonders if the judge will let her take over Heather's second speech. She's pretty sure Heather's got the first one down, but rebuttals … she knows this is ludicrous. You can't make your partner's speeches for her. All you can do is tell her to *quit gabbing to some guy and pay attention.*

Adlen knows she shouldn't, but that doesn't keep her from running over to where Heather stands, grabbing her arm, and saying: "We've got to get to our room. The round's starting."

"Let go of me," says Heather. "Geez, Addie, what are you doing?"

The guy is gone.

"We have work to do. We have to start working. We can't play around." Adlen's heart is beating too fast. She doesn't want to go to C105 where the round's starting. She wants to slip out the smooth double-doors and never come back. She's never been trapped this close to failure before.

"Relax," says Heather. "This isn't life or death. It's just a debate tournament. Geez," she says again, "why are you so desperate?"

"I'm not desperate," Adlen says. "I just have to be good at this."

"Why?" asks Heather. She makes it sound like a reasonable enough question.

"Why?" asks Adlen. "What do you mean, why? I need to win."

"No you don't," Heather says. "No one *needs* to win."

"I do," Adlen says. "I'm a natural." She thinks about Dad, his real smile. She thinks about the gift inside her. "Debate is my thing."

"Your 'thing'?" Heather repeats, and looks just skeptical enough to make Adlen stop hating her.

What Heather Must Know:

1. ~~Heather must not think she is smarter than Adlen. Adlen has been debating for over a year. Adlen attended an intensive six-week debate camp at Stanford over the summer. Heather lay by the pool reading *CosmoGirl!* over the summer.~~

2. ~~Heather must read the evidence when she responds to an argument. She cannot just tell the other team that they're wrong. Refus-~~

ing to read the evidence will result in a losing ballot.

3. Heather must understand their affirmative
plan. If she doesn't understand the plan, she
won't be able to give a convincing argument
for why the U.S. should adopt it. Adlen
knows the Plan and will answer any questions Heather has about the Plan.

4. Heather must know counter-plan theory.
The other team will likely run a counter-plan
against them, and Heather needs to attack it
correctly, or the other team will win.

5. Heather must learn about topicality arguments. As Adlen's dad, debate guru, always
says, topicality is the RFD debaters most
often overlook. Heather must know that
RFD is debate shorthand for "reason for
decision"—the reason judges decide to vote
for teams. Or against them. Judges cannot
vote against Adlen and Heather. Debate is
Adlen's thing.

6. She has to carry the tub.

American Forensic Association Debate Ballot

Division: Open Round: 1 Room: C105 Judge: Miller

Affirmative: Haven Negative: Sky Crest

Rank each debater in order of excellence (1 for best, 2 for next best, etc.).

1st Affirmative (name): Heather 1st Negative (name): Tyler
Rank: 4 Rank: 3

You're new, aren't you? Look, debate is
NOT about making the other team look
stupid (well, it is, but not in the way
you think). You need to make better
arguments. "Uh-Uh" is not an argument.
Adlen made all the right arguments in
her speech. BUT then you ignored them
and just rambled. You need to extend her
arguments and build on them. Just listen
to Adlen and try to do what she tells you. She really understands debate.

2nd Affirmative (name): Adlen 2nd Negative (name): James
Rank: 1 Rank: 2

You're a star! Keep it up. Nice job, neg.

In my opinion, the better debating was done by __The negative Team__ .
                                                        (Aff. or Neg.)

RFD: This was a hard round to judge. The negative team did a good job, but
Adlen was killing them. Then Heather just dropped too many arguments. Adlen
did her best and I wanted to vote for her, but there just wasn't enough there
in Heather's rebuttal.

                    Bill Miller
        _____
                JUDGE'S SIGNATURE

Dad is asleep when Adlen comes back from the tournament. This is unusual. Usually her dad is waiting up for her after a tournament, playing Red Alert on his laptop until she gets in. They discuss the teams she went up against, the arguments they made, whether the judges were idiots or not. But tonight she is surprised to see him lying back in his recliner, snoring softly, a football game muted on the TV.

She knows she could wake him, but she doesn't. The green fact-men have taken over her mind again, and she doesn't want to talk about losing. She wants to go to bed so her brain will stop moving.

On her way to the bathroom, she passes K.L.'s room. The light is on, even though she knows K.L. isn't home. He's never home on Friday nights. It is when she goes to turn out the light that she remembers K.L.'s notebook still in her backpack. She'll return it to him before bed.

Adlen brushes her teeth and goes into her room, where she has dropped her backpack on the bed. She is aware of herself unzipping the bag slowly, though she doesn't know why. She knows she should hurry and take the notebook to K.L.'s room. Then she should fall asleep. She knows what she should do.

When she takes the notebook out her heart gets hot. Not hot in an I-always-knew-debate-would-give-me-a-heart-attack way. Hot the way her heart feels when she has the Spirit. Hot the way her heart felt when she drew Claire.

The notebook falls open, to the pages with the crash course and the sketch of the marquee. She can see now how far from good both things are: the empty, meaningless words about trying to mold Heather into a competent debater; the meticulous, thoughtful drawing of Harry the Husky. She is scared to turn the page. What if the drawing of Claire is like that? What if it is worse, infinitely worse, than she remembers it? She imagines the hot, exhilarated feeling leaving her chest, and the sadness of it is almost enough to make her close the book right then.

Almost.

When she turns the page, she sees that it *is* good. She thought she'd feel relieved, but she doesn't. Relief is what she feels after placing first in a tournament, or winning a round, or finishing a speech. Her feeling now is an itch going through her whole body, an itch begging her to pick up a pencil and draw more. She feels the hot, happy itch and wants to keep it.

The green men have left her head. She realizes they left her head when she was drawing Claire, too. The green men have no place in a world where logic means nothing.

She thinks about Joel telling her how trapped she

looked during rebuttals. She didn't just look trapped; she was trapped. Joel was trapped, too, trapped by something bigger than debate. Adlen still doesn't know what it was, but she's thought about it over the last few months.

FACT: There wasn't enough water on the hike.

FACT: Joel didn't drink enough to stay alive.

Those facts alone mean nothing. Those facts alone aren't enough to hold up any kind of argument. But she thinks that maybe Joel *let* himself die. Maybe he was trapped and couldn't figure any other way out.

That's how you get when you're trapped: desperate.

She thinks about how she feels now: the opposite of relaxed, but the opposite of trapped, too. Deep inside her brain she knows it's impossible for one emotion to be the "opposite" of two completely different emotions. But she doesn't care.

It is time for her to give her closing argument.

Resolved: Adlen, in Keeping with the Status Quo, Continues Her Debate Career.

1. Adlen has demonstrated skill with debate techniques. She is able to understand and break down complex issues easily. This is her God-given gift.

2. When Adlen wins a debate tournament, she is proving to everyone that she has talent.

K.L. may be a super-jock, but she has something, too. She has debate.

3. Adlen's dad loves her and he loves debate. When he has both at the same time, Adlen can see the excitement shine through his eyes. She doesn't want to take that away from him.

Disadvantages to the Proposed Resolution:

1. Adlen doesn't like debate. She has skill with debate techniques, but she doesn't like using them. While she is able to break down complex debate issues easily, she is more interested in learning how to break down *real* issues easily. If our talents are gifts from God, must we use them no matter what? Do parents love some children more than others? Does God love his straight children more than his gay ones? Why do some people think he does? These are complex issues she can't break down or write down or wrap her head around. Debate doesn't help her find solutions—it just gives her facts.

Adlen's sick of facts.

Facts don't help.

Arguments don't help.

This doesn't help.

THIS DOESN'T HELP.

She's going to give the notebook back to K.L. She tears out the crash course, the drawing of Harry, the final argument. But she leaves the picture of Claire right where it is. She knows she will draw other portraits just as good.

Wednesday's child is full of woe.
SEPTEMBER 13

MILES

Think: You don't know shit.

Think: McGuire, you're seriously screwed.

It hits me as I'm sitting there in the Civic, watching a run-down white house like it's gonna go somewhere. What the hell am I doing? But I sit there still.

He lives on a dead end, a dead end that runs into a parking lot but not one for a business. There's just this big ugly building with a big empty parking lot. Probably it's a drug cartel—nobody ever goes in, nobody ever comes out. Probably there's this whole Haven meth ring going down in there but the cops are too stupid to realize it. No one tears it down, at least. So that's where I wait.

I hate to wait, and that's why it's a problem how I don't know shit. If I did, I'd know what time the kid gets home from school. I don't know, though. Lot of things I don't know.

Like I don't know why I'm doing this, waiting for this kid, and I don't know what I'm gonna do when I find him. I don't know why it's him I want to beat the shit out of when it's not his fault.

I know only that he reminds me of someone. Someone I want to keep hurting until I stop hurting.

Could be a long time.

The house looks different in the day. I've never seen it in daylight.

Remember: The first time.

I did it for Joel.

Calling up Harris, asking him to go egging. Harris, being the kind of guy who was stupid enough not to ask questions and smart enough not to ask questions, he said yes. So I picked him up in the Civ. I forgot the eggs. It was all good though, cause he had three dozen.

"Seriously, though, should I be wondering whose house this is?" Harris had a sweet arm from football, and he chucked an egg. It was dark out, but I heard the crunch when it made contact.

I didn't answer, and Harris didn't say anything. He kept throwing, and so did I. I could breathe easier, throwing.

I did it for Joel.

Joel had never been egging.

When I found that out I mocked him, bad.

We were all hanging out at Harris' place one Friday night. Harris thought Joel was a dweeb (that word exactly: "Dude, why are you hanging out with that kid? He's an old-school *dweeb*") but he let me bring Joel around. We were in Harris' kitchen, eating little plastic containers of chocolate pudding. It was late. We were bored.

When I was little my dad had this puzzle called a Rubik's Cube, and you rotated these colored blocks to try to solve it. I'd play with it for a while, then be all "this is lame." Twist it more, be like "This cube sucks." But I still couldn't put it down.

When me and Joel and Harris chilled together, it was like Harris was playing with a Rubik's Cube.

"Dude, let's go egging!" said Harris, licking the last of the pudding off a foil lid. It was Harris' answer to everything.

Joel's eyes got wide. "It's against the law," he said.

Every time I mocked Joel, he'd brought it on himself. Other people mocked him behind his back and that wasn't cool. I had to let people know what was up with that; that I wasn't gonna hear it. And people knew their place around me. They gave me respect, so they gave Joel respect, too. But every time *I* mocked him, it was because he totally brought it on.

"It's against the law," I said, using the same voice I used to imitate Norah.

"I'm serious, you guys. You really egg people's houses? Doesn't that damage the paint?"

"That's on *cars*," said Harris, and he rolled his eyes. "Joel, dude, this is pathetic. You've gotta egg someone at least once."

Joel looked from me to Harris and back to me.

I nodded. "Yeah, it's a rite of passage for guys. Of course, most guys are like, twelve, when it happens."

This made Harris bust up. Something about the combination of sugar and nothing to do made him the Mormon equivalent of drunk.

"Come on," I said to Joel. "Be a man."

"You gotta learn the finer points of egging," said

Harris all seriously. Then he started losing it again. A glob of pudding dripped out of his nose like thick snot. "Like, first you decide who you wanna get."

"I don't want to get anyone," said Joel. He was looking at a patchwork wall-hanging over Harris' head that read: *Blessed are the "Piece" makers.*

"Well, who's pissing you off?" asked Harris

Joel's muscles tensed up—in his shoulders, in his face. He hated it when people used "bad language." Joel considered half of regular people's vocabulary "bad language."

"No one," he said, and he was Joel again, smiling with those freckles and that Nice Guy face. "Nobody's bugging me."

"What about a girl? You got a girl you're mad at?" asked Harris. "Or a girl you like?"

Joel's eyes got wide, and he was setting himself up again. "You egg people you like?"

"Maybe not egg 'em," I said. "But maybe TP her house."

"Yeah, you got a girl you wanna toilet paper?" Harris looked at Joel with his glassy, sugar-drunk eyes.

Joel played with the edge of the tablecloth, rubbing the fabric between his thumb and his forefinger. "No, not really. What about you?"

Harris put up his hands, like *whoa, step back.* "Hey, we aren't talking about me, here. I've been TPing before."

"Who is she?" I asked Joel. "You never told me there was a girl."

Once, back before Lissa and I were together, the three of us were playing HORSE and Lissa came up with this idea that if me or Joel won, she'd kiss the winner, and if she won she got to choose one of us to kiss her. I was game, because back then Lissa wasn't this needy girlfriend, she was some hot girl who was way better at making baskets than Joel. But Joel went ballistic, all about how he wasn't gonna date before he was sixteen, let alone kiss a girl. And I was like, "Dude, WTF? Are you gay? It's just a kiss." Then he got on this trip that until he was sixteen girls and guys were just the same to him, and same as he would never kiss a guy before he was sixteen he would never kiss a girl because guys and girls were just the same to him: friends only.

I wanted to let him know that was totally jacked up, but more than that I wanted him to shut up and play, so the deal was off and I stopped talking to him about girls.

But then he did turn sixteen, and I figured all those years of deprivation would have turned him into this sex-crazed maniac, but nothing. He never even talked about girls. He never told me there was a girl.

But now there was, cause Joel said, "There's no girl," and it was easy to tell he was lying. Even Harris caught it.

"Let's TP her house," said Harris. "Start out with something easy, something that isn't dangerous. TPing, there's no thrill, except thinking she might come out and see you."

"And she might not be wearing many clothes," I said to make Joel blush, which he did.

"Yeah, like just a T-shirt," said Harris.

"And no bra," I said. "And it might be cold out…"

"Shut up!" Joel threw his pudding cup at me, and it set Harris off. He started singing, "Ooh noo, a pudding cup" in this really bad falsetto, and no doubt about it: he was stone-cold-sober drunk.

"Okay, fine," said Joel, putting on his game face. "I tell you, we go TP her house, then you guys give it up, okay?"

Me and Harris nodded okay.

Joel picked up his pudding cup from where it had fallen right under my chair, and threw it in the garbage. He was gonna make me wait for this. He was enjoying it. So was I, kind of.

"Norah," he said. "I like Norah. So let's go."

"Norah who?" said Harris.

Joel ignored him.

I did, too. "Dude, no way I'm toilet papering Norah."

"Why not?" Joel asked.

"Because it's retarded to TP your own house," I said, ignoring Joel's thing about language.

"Your house?" said Harris. "This chick lives at your house?"

"Harris, clue in," I said. "Norah's my little sister, man. Joel wants to TP my little sister."

"Sick," said Harris. "Not in a good way. Sick like disturbed."

"You guys said you would do it," Joel said, getting up from the table, grabbing his coat off the back of the chair. "So let's do it."

"He's got a point," said Harris, and I was wishing that Harris hadn't chosen this moment to start understanding logic.

I grabbed a stash of toilet paper from the year's supply of everything that Harris' mom kept in the storage room downstairs. Joel just kept looking at me with this annoying *I-told-you-so* look. But I couldn't figure out what it meant. Told me not to bug him to go TPing or he'd find a way to get back at me? Or did he actually like Norah? Had he told me that and I'd somehow missed it?

No. He'd never told me that. I'd remember. "Dude, are you really hot for Norah?"

Joel was carrying a twenty-four pack of Cottonelle. "What do you think?" he asked, and followed Harris out the back door.

Thing was, I didn't know what I thought.

Was that why Joel never talked about girls? He liked Norah?

Sick as it sounded, part of me hoped he did.

"I feel like a jackass," I said. We were all in Harris' Acura with the lights off.

"Shut up," said Harris.

"I'm TPing my own house," I complained.

"Shut *up*," said Harris and Joel together.

We drove up to the side road next to my condo complex, stupidly named "El Casa Fantastico" by an even stupider developer. All that separated the street from my condo was a chain-link fence, so we had to get in and out before anyone saw us. A huge risk, in a place like El Casa Craptastico.

"We better make this quick," I said, running my finger under that first fresh layer of paper, tearing it so it was ready to roll. No pun intended. "If my mom catches me vandalizing my own house, I'm screwed."

"Relax, McGuire, we'll be quick." Harris cut the engine. "Okay, Joel, you know what to do?"

"Uh, throw the toilet paper?" he said. "Any techniques I should know about?"

I couldn't see his face to tell if he was kidding or not.

"Do it fast and use up as much paper as you can," Harris said.

I sighed. "Let's just get this over with."

I didn't want to toilet paper my condo, not just because it was my condo, but because it was *my condo*. My condo with practically no yard. My condo with condos in front of it and more condos behind it. My condo that would take two seconds to toilet paper. I was just glad no lights were on anywhere near us.

Harris was a heavy-footed runner but fast from football, and he was in the backyard in no time. He had stuffed about a million rolls under his letterman jacket, and he was holding the bottom of his jacket like a baby so they wouldn't roll out.

"Ready?" I asked Joel. The inside light from the car was still on and I could see Joel's eyes, all shiny and excited, and I finally got it: that punk kid liked my sister. WTF?

Joel said, "I was born ready," and took off. I looked at him, with his one measly roll in each hand, and closed the Acura door and the light went off.

He hadn't wanted to tell me. And I had to give him respect for that. He didn't want it to change things, or whatever. He was being Mr. Nice Guy, not all "hey, buddy, I want to bang your baby sister, is that cool?"

Was it supposed to be weird if your best friend wanted your sister? It didn't feel weird. It felt like something that had been weird that wasn't anymore.

My eyes had adjusted to the dark and dude, Joel had no idea how to TP. My "yard," like all the rest at El Casa, had this ghetto picket fence around it and Joel was tearing off lengths of paper and tossing them over each post. Harris, with his awesome arm, was hucking rolls over the roof—which was technically also the neighbor's roof, but whatever.

I'd be the one cleaning it up in the morning anyway. Probably someone would drag me out of bed to undo what I'd done. Why not do it? Why not let Joel know I was cool with it, him liking Norah? That I was cool with whatever?

I scaled the picket fence and decorated the tiny bushes that were dying, and wrapped the little bench that everybody was so proud of just cause it was the first thing we bought for our new place without Dad. I looked up from the stupid bench, wrapped good and tight.

Harris must have been on the other side of the condo, because rolls were flying toward me. So I cocked my arm, too, letting the roll spiral into the sky, heavy. I imagined it coming down like Harris' roll, floating like it was nothing, with not a problem in sight.

Harris was talking nonstop once we were all back in the Acura. "Dude, that was so sweet! Sooo sweet! I forgot what a rush that is."

Paper stretched from one side of the roof to the other. It waved like flags from each post on the fence. There wasn't much wind, and I hoped it wouldn't pick up during the night and blow those off. I wanted Norah to see them. Dude, I didn't even *like* Norah. But I wanted her to see them.

Joel said, "Yeah, it was amazing." He cleared his throat and I could feel him looking at me. "Next time let's go egging, okay?"

"Yeeee-haw!" said Harris, taking his hands off the wheel and pumping his fists like it was a huge victory.

Next time turned out to be that time. The first time.

I did it for Joel.

It's risky, but I gotta turn the car on.

The sun's coming at me from every direction and keeping the windows open is doing jack for keeping me cool. I need AC, and I need it bad. The neighborhood's been dead since I got here, so I just pray it stays that way and turn the key in the ignition.

Cool air hits me and it wakes me up some, but I still don't dare turn on the CD player. Times like this I need an iPod like everybody else on the planet. Times like this I remember that if I could afford an iPod, I could probably afford to live anywhere else besides El Casa Craptastico.

Sunlight splinters from the crack in the Civ's windshield.

A couple months ago I went back. Not to be all stalker or anything, but I had to see my old house, where we'd lived with my dad. It was like everything was gone, and I had to go home to prove that I had something once. When I got there, some crazy-ass statue was in the front yard where the tree used to be.

I hated that tree. My dad, Master Gardener, had

planted it one day just for kicks. The guy next door had been pissed because it was totally the wrong type of tree to plant. Even though it cracked me up to see the guy losing it over some tree, there was no getting around how ugly it was and how wrong it looked.

But that statue was worse.

So I drove back to El Casa, fast on the freeway 'cause it was far away, and a rock flew up and hit the windshield, passenger side. I knew I should fix it but it just never happened, and the chip kept growing, and now there's this line spanning from one side to the other.

The house looks different in the daylight, but there's something else not quite right. Something else is missing. The Tacoma.

There's no Tacoma in the driveway. He must be driving it. Bastard.

Remember: The second time.

The usual: driving down the dark streets, no music on, no noise outside. Just me driving: into the parking lot, flipping a U-turn, driving back out past his house. The house was pure dark. No one awake. It was two o'clock in the morning so I didn't expect them to be, but there wasn't even a porch light on. The house was washed in the leftover light from the cartel parking lot.

I saw nothing but that stupid Toyota Tacoma, the dark green blending into the darkness that was over everything.

I hated that Tacoma.

I thought, *Doesn't he? Doesn't Brother Smith think of Joel every time he drives that stupid truck?*

If it was my truck, I wouldn't drive it. If I were stupid enough to leave my Toyota Tacoma out in the open where anyone could take it, without even a porch light on, I wouldn't be surprised if someone else drove away in it.

I could've hotwired it if I'd wanted to; a guy taught me how to back in junior high and I still remembered.

But I didn't want to take it. I didn't want to drive that truck. I didn't want anyone to drive that truck ever again. I hated that truck like I hated Brother Smith, and I hated how when I saw it I saw how everything started, with Joel reading the map and Brother Smith whistling and me leaning against the window, and I couldn't believe he could still drive it.

I didn't take the truck. But me and Joel's pocketknife, we made sure nobody drove it for a long, long time.

That was the second time.

I did it for Joel.

I check the clock and it's 2:57, late enough that somebody's gonna be strolling down the street soon. It better be Brother Smith Junior. I'll know that kid when I see him. I've seen him before.

He was there when we left for the hike, sitting on the back of a Dodge 4x4, letting his skinny, punk legs dangle from the edge. He kept complaining about how he couldn't go because he was only thirteen, but he should get to go because he'd be fourteen next month.

Like it was gonna change anything because he was sitting there whining. Like his dad was gonna be all, "you're right, son, screw the rules and forget that we're leaving right now. Let's stop everything and go pack your stuff so you can come annoy the hell out of us for the whole trip."

Bastard. I wish he *had* gone on the hike. I wish *he'd* been the one to give away his water. Maybe if his kid had been the one to die, Brother Smith wouldn't go around driving his Tacoma like everything was fine.

I see Joel's pocketknife glint red on the dashboard, and I know what I'm gonna do. I'm not gonna send the kid to the ER. Or maybe I will. But me and Joel's pocketknife, we're gonna take care of it. We're gonna make it stop hurting.

I didn't even want to go.

Hiking the Grand Canyon with the Boy Scouts? Completely lame-A.

It was my mom who made me. She heard about it because some lady she knew from Relief Society was married to the Scoutmaster.

I wasn't at church that morning. I was at home trying to sleep. My sister had just moved back home. And her two kids. Far as I could tell, other kids liked to play with toys, but these kids liked to make noise.

First thing I heard Sunday morning? More noise. Not from the kids. From Mom. All about how I was never at church anymore and the school had been calling and what I needed was some discipline. All about how she couldn't give it to me and my father was never going to come back and give it to me, so maybe I could get it on this trip. From the Scoutmaster. Brother Smith.

I knew arguing would make her madder, but if I played along she'd forget about it.

She didn't.

Two weeks later, at too-early-o'clock in the morning, she actually drove me to the church herself. Joel, all chipper and *how-can-I-help?* showed me where to load my stuff. Into a dark green Tacoma. Me, Joel and Brother Smith, on the open road.

And then I've got nothing.

Before I could leave the hospital I had to talk to this counselor, who supposedly "specialized in helping teens." She was wearing a black skirt, long enough to be conservative but short enough to distract me, and that was about it for help.

She wanted me to tell her what I remembered about the "accident" and I told her I couldn't remember anything after leaving the church. It was mostly true, but I thought for sure she'd think I was lying.

She didn't. She went on and on about how that was natural, how they were doing all this research on post-traumatic stress disorder and sometimes people couldn't remember the event, and on and on about the hippocampus and whatever. I just wanted a discharge.

Because now I knew *she* was lying. I knew about post-traumatic stress disorder enough from health class to know it was when you remembered something too well. How could you have the opposite symptoms but still the same disease? Obviously, it was bullshit.

I remembered stuff about traumatic events. I remembered my dad leaving, how he was becoming some born-again Buddhist-Nazi and gave me this pamphlet called "The Greatest Lie Ever Told" the day he moved out. As if I, at fourteen years old, gave a shit why he was leaving. I just cared that he was leaving.

And I remembered when I was over at Abuelita's one time as a kid, reading to her. Me and Abuelita, we had this bond-thing going. She loved the Chronicles of Narnia and we were in the middle of page forty-three of *The Magician's Nephew* when she had her stroke. After that she couldn't even say my name.

So how come I almost died and I can only remember part of it? How come there's only this one scene, playing over and over, and nothing else? How come I remember that the pamphlet had a big question mark on it, with a bunch of clouds all around it, but I can't remember why there wasn't enough water and why I let Joel give his away instead of drink it?

All I remember:

Seeing the river. Trying to run but I couldn't. Too tired.

Joel was worse, though. Joel was barely even walking, just swaying back and forth.

But I could see the river. I was all: "Come on, man." Talking hurt.

Joel just smiled, sorta. His eyes were all sunken in and it was a smile that didn't look like one. "My pocket knife is in my pocket."

He was delirious. Shit. He was delirious. He needed water. "I see the river," I said. "We're almost there."

"Get my pocketknife out of my pocket," he said. "I want you to have it, Miles. I want you to have it to remember me. I love you." It was all slurred and mumbled.

"Yeah, okay," I said, and then Joel collapsed, hard, and he hit his head when he fell. There wasn't much blood, just a thin line down his face, so I thought, that's a good sign, right? Not much blood?

Then his eyes rolled back and forth and his breathing got fast. Really fast and I could hear him take each breath. That was a good sign, right? That he was still breathing?

"I'm going to get water," I said. "Just hold on."

"Knife," slurred Joel. "Take the knife."

When I see the kid at first I think it's a mirage from the heat. I think I'm imagining the figure walking this direction. But no. He's really here. I thought about him and it made him show up, like I have some magic power. Like I'm greater than myself. It'd be so easy to go out there, larger than life, with the knife and get in the kid's face.

So I do. The kid's alone. I expected that. And he looks nervous seeing me walk toward him. I expected that. And I get closer and his jeans are way too short and I expected that, too. And I get closer and I flip up the blade on the knife and his eyes get round. I see fear. I expected that.

And I see his hair, parted to the side, like a mama's boy.

Seeing him, I don't think: Brother Smith.

I think: *Joel.*

I think: Joel's forgiven Brother Smith.

I know: Joel probably never even blamed Brother Smith in the first place.

But I'm not like Joel. Never said I was.

I met Joel the day after I moved into El Casa Craptastico.

I wasn't up for church, but Mom was all *we're going to church today as a family* and I knew her almost-crying voice and that was it. So I put on a white shirt and the tie Norah gave me and I knew it would make 'em all happy and it did. Making people happy was easy. Comb a part in my hair for Mom. Put some gel in it for the ladies. Slick it back for basketball with the guys. No problem.

The kids in the ward weren't bad. Me and Norah were the only ones from the condos, but no one gave us crap about it. I just smiled a lot and girls were all over me and pretty soon guys were coming over, too, slapping me high fives and asking how my hook shot was.

I had a dad who was MIA, groceries from the government, and a piece of crap pretending to be a house. But I had mad basketball skills and a good smile and that was keeping everybody happy. It was gonna be okay.

There was this one kid I noticed because he was the only one who didn't like me yet.

He was cleaning up—putting away hymnbooks and stacking folding chairs. His hair was parted on the side, like mine, but he looked like the kind of mama's boy who kept it that way all the time. He wore a well-fitting navy blue suit instead of a white shirt and khakis like the other guys. WTF? He was wearing a *tie tack*. The kid posed no threat. If he didn't like me it'd be okay.

Except then he looked at me. He looked at me longer than guys look at each other. The kid looked at me, looked through me, and he knew.

He knew I used to be a good kid, once. Maybe he knew how I read to my grandma back then and made people happy cause I wanted to, not cause I had to. But he knew it wasn't that way now.

He could tell I was just playing a game during the

day, but at night I became the person I really was. Probably he knew I had dreams about beating the crap out of people—that annoying kid from *7th Heaven*, last year's bio teacher, my dad. Every night I hit people until they bled; watched them die.

It scared me, knowing what that kid knew. But it was a relief, too. Because I spent all day everyday trying to keep everybody happy so they wouldn't figure out what a bad kid I'd become. This kid? This kid I could never fool. Just wasn't how it was gonna be. However he knew me, he knew me, and that was a load off my mind.

As long as he was on my side.

He leaned the last chair up against the wall and walked up to me. I was going crazy wondering what he was gonna say, 'cause I could tell it was something.

The groups around me buzzed off one by one, saying see you in school or at church ball on Wednesday. I kept happy-face and nodded bye, all cool, but half my look was at the kid coming toward me still. Thinking: what's he gonna say? Thinking: he could change things for me. Thinking: please be cool.

He looked at me and he had freckles. Freckles and I was scared? Freckles and I was relieved? How could a kid with freckles mess me up this bad? So I said, "'Sup?"

And he nodded and went: "Nice hair."

He wasn't the type to be slamming me, but *nice hair?* WTF? So I was like, "Nice hair yourself."

He just smiled and said: "I like it this way."

Thing was, I knew he did, but I didn't know him. So I said: "What's your name, anyway?"

"Joel," he said. "What's yours?"

"Miles," I told him. "Miles McGuire."

He thought it over and said: "It fits you."

WTF? *It fits you?*

"Keep the name," he said. "But change the hair."

And I opened my mouth, but I couldn't say anything.

Other people I'd tell to shut up, or shut the hell up, depending. Or I'd walk away and be like, "Freak." But I just stared at him, at his sorry freckled face and mama's boy hair. And I knew him. And he knew me. And something started that was like a shiver, but I stopped it right then 'cause I wasn't a guy who shivered.

And seconds went by, but I still couldn't say anything.

Finally, he said: "You wanna chill? We're having family game night, and you're invited."

"Family game night?" I said. "WTF?"

"Don't swear."

"Dude, it's not swearing. Swearing would be if I said what the—"

"Let's just go," he said.

And it was like I had known all along I'd say yes, and he'd known all along I'd say yes, but I was still surprised to hear myself say okay.

I'm not like Joel, but I flip the blade back in. I stand face to face with that kid, except that he's so short I'm still staring him down, even though that's not how I want it to be. Not anymore.

But the kid's still shaking. I just watch him shake for a sec, seeing how he doesn't run, doesn't say anything, just shakes. Idiot kid looks like he's having a seizure.

He's a dumbass. So's his dad.

But it doesn't matter. I still know what I've gotta say.

So I do. I tell the kid: "He forgives him, man. He forgives him."

The kid looks at me still and I look at him. Why it hurts I don't know, but it does.

So I turn around.

Next thing I know, the Civic is driving itself to the nursing home on Sycamore. I go in and a nurse is asking if she can help me, and I'm asking where Maria Luisa's room is.

I've never been to see Abuelita.

She doesn't know who I am, anyway.

But who does? So I might as well go in.

Abuelita is sleeping. She is very old and her room smells like ammonia and food and a disgusting meat smell. I want to leave, but instead I sit on a hard plastic chair near her bed, and I hold her hand, with its shriveled veins poking into my young ones.

"I slashed a guy's tires, Abuelita," I say. "Today

I almost beat up his son. I was mad. He let my best friend die."

Abuelita just goes on sleeping.

"I can't believe I slashed a guy's tires. I can't believe I almost beat up his son. I used to be a good kid, didn't I?"

Abuelita's eyes move, and then open. "Miles," she says. "Miles Anthony."

My name. She knows my name. She recognizes me.

I remember how it used to be, when Abuelita looked at me. Like I was the best kid in the whole world. No matter if I had a buzz cut or a baseball hat, I was handsome. No matter if I could stomach some of that gross Peruvian drink she made or not, I was a good boy. Maybe to her, I still am.

"Miles," she says again. She grips my pinkie. "Miles Anthony."

Take a breath; a deep one.

Say: "*Soy yo*, Abuelita."

Tell her: "It's just me."

Thursday's child has far to go.

CLAIRE

It was the morning of the day I decided to leave.

I wanted to get from the pick-up/drop-off zone of the parking lot, where I was currently standing, to the glass doors to Haven High, but the steady stream of cars heading into the A-lot was making it impossible.

I was thinking about my worries, counting them like beads on a rosary. Okay, so I'd never actually seen a rosary before, and I wasn't sure what you actually did when you counted on one, but I'd heard about it in a song once. I imagined my rosary like one of those slidey-bead toys in doctors' waiting rooms, where you move the bead from one side of a twisty wire to the other.

Bead one: I was going to be late to class, because I went to school with a bunch of overprivileged white kids rocking out in new Toyotas and clearly not yielding to pedestrians.

But that was just the beginning.

I tried to pull the short sleeves of my pink T-shirt away from my armpits without someone noticing. Already I was sweaty and hot. It was a day in late September, a piece of autumn, and it was supposed to get up to ninety degrees. What right had a piece of autumn to get up to ninety degrees?

That's when I heard a car honk.

It was from a silver Miata, driven by one Natalie Summerson, stopped right in front of me. She waved me across the street with the back of her hand.

I did not make eye contact with Natalie. I walked.

I wished I had a silver Miata. Not because I wanted a silver Miata, or even a car, but because I wanted to go away. If I had a silver Miata I would drive. I would drive far, far away from this town. Far away from everybody who knew me or might ever know me if I stayed here. If I had a silver Miata, I would drive and I would not talk to a single living soul. I would talk to Joel and not look over my shoulder to see who was listening. I would not worry about who was thinking what about me talking to a dead guy. I would talk to Joel and he would be dead—he would know it and I would know it—but still it would be like old times, kind of.

I wished I had a silver Miata.

But I didn't even have a license.

Bead two: I didn't know how to drive.

Haven High is carpeted, not just the floors but the walls, too, so when I walked in it already felt and smelled like a sweat sock. Since I was running late from the whole getting-into-school debacle, I skipped going to my locker and cut through the cafeteria. My driver's ed class was on the other side of the building.

I couldn't get Natalie Summerson and her silver Miata out of my head. It wasn't her fault that she'd moved to a new "gated hillside community" down the street from her posh old house in Knob Farms, and it wasn't her fault that my family had bought it. But still.

I hated living in Natalie Summerson's old room. It felt like wearing somebody else's underwear.

Natalie Summerson's old house was bigger than our old one on Maple Street. There were five bathrooms. There were two living rooms, as though we intended to do twice the living we did in our old house. There was a swimming pool in the backyard.

On the rosary of my sucky life, that was bead three: I lived in a house that wasn't really mine.

By the time I reached the classroom it was almost time for the bell to ring, so I wasn't the only one at the door. I arrived at the precise moment Tate Williams did.

Tate Williams, Golden Boy of Haven High. Tate Williams, a guy who was no doubt getting a new Prius or Matrix for his sixteenth birthday. Tate Williams, the guy who made most girls want to swoon and me want to spit. I took a step back.

"After you, Claire," said Tate, smiling at me and gesturing to the door.

Tate Williams, smiling at me? Tate Williams, knowing my name? What was that all about?

And could this day blow any harder?

Answer: yes.

I walked in as the bell blasted, and scooted into a seat as Mr. Cramblitt, the driver's ed teacher/basketball coach, was saying: "I need release forms from those of you who'll be driving today: Claire Espen, Tucker Frye,

Mason Grant, and Shelby Holloway. Please bring them to the front with you. The rest of you, study your driving handbook."

I took the release form out of my folder. I'd had to forge the signature. Mom was always asleep lately, or "out to lunch," which totally took on a new meaning with her. They shouldn't let depressed people have kids. When tragedy strikes, people who are tragic to begin with totally can't handle it. At least Dad had an excuse for checking out: he was always working, probably earning the extra money for the extra living room.

I knew I could say my form wasn't signed, get out of it completely (this school wouldn't even let you eat a peanut without your parents' permission), but that would cause even more problems. All I wanted to do was get this over with.

Joel had been teaching me how to drive. Last February I'd been freaking out about actually turning *sixteen* in less than a year—in Haven and West Haven alike, it's a magical birthday. I guess it is most places. But in Haven/West Haven, and any place else where the Mormon population sits at around 94 percent, sixteen is something extra. Sixteen is dating age.

I was worried about the dating, but more about the driving.

"Relax," Joel had said. He was eating Cheetos and there was a thin line of neon-orange powder above his upper lip. I wondered if he had done it on purpose. You could never tell, with Joel. "I'll teach you to drive."

"*You* will?" I said. "Isn't that what driver's ed is for?"

"You gotta know how to drive before you get into driver's ed, Claire, else you're gonna look stupid." He crunched down on another Cheeto, and I watched it dissolve in his mouth while he talked.

Disgusting.

"Let's go. Get your shoes. You always wear shoes when you drive."

"Now?" I said. I was fifteen and a few months. I didn't have a permit.

Joel read my mind—he could do that, and not just with me. "Don't worry about it. We'll go down to the church parking lot. I'll get my keys."

Joel didn't even have to ask if we could go. He could use the car whenever he wanted without permission. Joel got privileges I didn't—he could stay out later, and he was best friends with Miles, a guy Mom and Dad didn't even like me to be around. Total double standard, and it annoyed me big-time. But then he was always using his powers for good, like Superman, so what could I say?

We went into the mudroom just off the kitchen. I put on my hiking boots with the good soles, just in case. We had just gotten a second dose of winter: more snow, more cold. Joel grabbed a BYU sweatshirt and a set of keys off the hook that had his name on a piece of masking tape above it. Mom had labeled one hook for each of us; the masking tape with my name had peeled off when I was little, so that the only part left was a sliver of the "a."

We drove to the back of the church, next to the dumpster and the satellite dish, and he moved the shift lever to "P."

Joel helped me adjust the seat and all the mirrors, told me when I pushed too hard on the brake, and made me stick my left foot behind me so I'd stop using it. He set up imaginary lanes for me ("Pretend you have to drive between that yellow line there and that white one on the side ... okay, if this was a real road, then you'd be hitting a car ... again, you'd be hitting a car ... another car, Claire, straighten your wheel ...") and helped me to park and reverse.

"You ready to drive around the whole church?" he asked. His eyes were gleaming. "Ready?"

Heck no, I wanted to say. *I'm ready to go home.*

I was ready to go home. I didn't want to practice anymore. But Joel was in his Superman mode. Joel looked like me—a skinny, short kid with pale hair and pale skin—but it was like he saw himself as something else entirely. He was always rescuing people, whether or not they really needed rescuing; whether or not he could really help them. It was how he was.

He got into Superman mode and sometimes it embarrassed me to no end, like when Dakota, the four-year-old next door, lost her cat, KitKat. Joel spearheaded this whole crusade to look for KitKat and put up fliers and everything, but by the time he finished, the cat had come home on her own. Dakota just looked at him with these big, dark eyes, and it was obvious she had forgotten that KitKat had even been missing.

But sometimes I just wanted to let him be Superman. So I said, "Okay, I'm ready to drive around the whole church," even though I really wasn't.

Since then, I'd never driven a car without him. But in a matter of minutes that's what I would be doing.

My T-shirt was getting wetter underneath my arms as I made my way to the front of the classroom. Everybody else was already there. I knew Shelby from West Haven Junior High, and I recognized one of the guys from church—Tucker. He was in the Knob Farms 2nd Ward, same as I was now.

Not that I expected him to know me. Or acknowledge me. After all, I had only attended Knob Farms 2nd Ward three times so far. I'd lived in Haven less than a month. So why did he say: "Hey, Claire," and lift his hand for a high five?

Since when had high fives been cool? Since when had it been cool for Tucker Frye, Knob Farms hotshot, to high-five Claire Espen, formerly of West Haven, the wrong side of the tracks? Were he and Tate Williams in on some kind of conspiracy?

The Goldens of Haven, conspiring against me. That was so bead four.

To be safe, I slapped Tucker's hand, careful not to raise my arm high enough to show the wet splotch.

Mr. White, the teacher who took us out driving, walked in. I wondered how they decide which teachers get to show films like *Mental Health When You're in the Driver's Seat* and which have to risk their lives on a daily basis. "Everybody got release forms?" he asked.

Geez, what is it with this school and release forms? We nodded.

"Okay, then follow me." The four of us headed into the hall, out the doors no one uses, and onto the driver's ed range. "We're taking this car. Frye, you first."

Tucker nodded and opened the front door. The car was nice—a white sedan that looked brand new. For some reason I thought they would have had us practice on something older—something you wouldn't feel bad about wrecking. My heart beat fast.

I was surprised when Tucker drove around the range like a pro. How did he become like a regular driver? This was his first time driving for real, wasn't it?

Mr. White said: "Okay, Frye, let's get out of here. Take a right onto Dandelion."

Dandelion? A major road? I considered asking why the rest of us didn't get to practice on the range, but then I surveyed the car: Shelby was smiling and Mason was nodding his head.

Probably wise not to say anything.

Turning right onto Dandelion meant you were heading toward West Haven, and Tucker drove around neighborhoods I hadn't seen all summer. Like the big falling-apart Victorian house that belonged to Sister Scott, who gave out caramel popcorn balls every Halloween. Parents never cared that they weren't pre-packaged. Everybody knew Sister Scott; knew she loved kids but never had had any of her own.

Or Grampa Bob's, the super-cheap grocery store we'd walk to on summer days to buy the Popsicles you suck out of little plastic pouches. Passing these places was weird, like watching a movie set or a place you once visited, or going through pictures from when you were young and seeing toys you forgot how much you loved.

"Okay," said Mr. White, writing something on his clipboard. "Holloway, you next."

Shelby and Tucker traded places. Tucker smelled like some kind of cologne and it made me sneeze. I tried to sneeze softly, but I just sneezed again. Then again.

I *would* be allergic to cologne. Bead number five.

Shelby started driving into Haven. I watched her make tight turns and drive the speed limit and check her blind spot. She was driving along the Haven streets, near the spa and the gym and the Barnes & Noble, and she was doing a good job.

Shelby, West Havenite, fit this town better than I did.

I sneezed again, then again, then again.

Mr. White gave Shelby a series of directions that took us into Knob Farms, with its three-car garages, lots of stucco, and my new neighborhood. Yippee.

"Pull over, Holloway," said Mr. White. "Espen, get up here."

Yes sir! I decided not to say. My heart beat fast again. I wasn't ready yet. I wanted to get it over with, but I wasn't ready. Not yet.

It would be okay. I would stare only at what was directly in front of me, and it would be okay.

I knew I was supposed to adjust the seat, but I couldn't find the lever, so I just felt around for a few seconds and buckled my seat belt. I pulled the rearview mirror down.

Mr. White stared at me. He looked kind of like the guy on my mom's old *Sweatin' to the Oldies* videos. Only with beadier eyes. "You want to adjust your seat?"

"No, I'm good," I said. "All ready."

I put on my blinker to pull into the road and started driving. Was I going fast enough? I pushed on the gas pedal lightly, which didn't do anything, and then I pushed harder, which did too much and lurched us forward. The car made a growling noise.

Mr. White wrote something on his clipboard.

Making sure the red marker stayed on the speedometer's twenty-five mph line was a full-time job. How could you do other stuff, too? Why didn't Joel and I practice how to go the speed limit?

Luckily, at this time of day the streets in Knob Farms were deserted, so at the stop sign I didn't have to stop all the way—making it easier to get back up to twenty five without that car-growl coming back.

"Rolling stop," said Mr. White, like I was supposed to know what that was and be shocked about it.

"I'm sorry?" I said, which I figured he could either interpret as I'm-sorry-there's-a-rolling-stop or I'm-sorry-but-I-don't-know-what-you're-talking-about, depending on what he wanted it to mean.

"You didn't come to a complete stop there."

I was on a street with no people. I was trying to keep the car from growling at me like an angry rottweiler. And all he cared about was that I hadn't come to a complete stop? "Sorry," I said.

"Sorry doesn't cut it in driving." He made another mark on his clipboard. "Don't look at me. Look at the road."

I dug my fingernails into the padded steering wheel. I wished I wasn't here. I wished I was in biology right now.

"Make a U-turn anywhere along this road."

U-turn.

Joel was going to teach me to do that.

I kept driving.

"Did you hear me? Just anywhere along here."

I saw plenty of places where I *couldn't* make a U-turn. First, the road started to narrow. Then I saw a car parked on one side of the road and another car parked on the other side of the road, so it wouldn't work there, either.

I couldn't make the U-turn. I wasn't ready. Every place I came to wouldn't work. It wouldn't work. If I tried to make the turn, it wouldn't work. I dug my nails deeper into the wheel.

"Are you planning to make the turn or not?"

I couldn't answer him. I kept staring at the road directly in front of me. If I just concentrated on the road directly in front of me...

"Pull over, Espen. You're done."

Even though I was done, he wasn't ("You call that pulling over? You're still in the middle of the road, Espen!"). I slunk into the newly vacated seat.

"I don't know how to make a U-turn, either," Shelby whispered. "I was practicing with my mom once? She said U-turns are hard when you're first learning."

When I got back to school there was only one place left to go. My haven from Haven: the faculty women's restroom. No one checked who went in there, and I'd never seen a teacher go in, either.

The faculty women's room had normal light, not fluorescent, and hearts stenciled on the wall. It smelled like citrus hand soap. It always had paper towels. There was never anyone else there.

I turned on the faucet. "Joel?" I whispered, even though I knew nobody was listening or could hear me even if they were. I looked into the mirror. It was gold-plated. I waited until I saw Joel's face, and when I did, I smiled. "The driver's ed car hates me," I told him. "I suck at driving."

Joel didn't even say something Joelish back, like "Give it a chance!" or "I bet you'll be a great driver with practice!" He just nodded and said, "I was going to teach you."

"I know," I said, but this time when I looked in the mirror I couldn't see his face looking back at me.

Today he wasn't staying as long as he usually did. It felt like a sign, but of course I didn't know what it was a sign of. I was just some nutcase who talked to her dead brother and didn't know how to drive. Deeper meaning was obviously over my head. "You picked a really bad time to die, you know," I told him.

But Joel was long gone.

I turned off the water and walked out of the rest-room. The new light was harsh and burned my eyes. I walked down the halls, backpack squarely on both shoulders, head up, chest out, determined to go home.

I couldn't stay. My eyes were still burning in the back and I knew what that meant: at any minute, the most random incident could set me off. The last thing I needed at this school was a rep as a rags-to-riches cry-baby who couldn't make a U-turn. I pushed my way out through the same stupid glass double doors I'd spent the better part of the morning trying to get in through.

Life, *my* life, was full of pathetic ironies like that.

"Hey, Claire, wait up!"

I knew that voice. It was Madison.

Madison. Bead six.

Madison and I weren't the kind of life-long best friends everybody thinks of when they think of life-long best friends. We didn't wear each other's pants or anything. It was just that we'd grown up next door to each other and we had lemonade stands in the summer and we always picked each other for science fair projects.

Technically, we were still best friends, even though we didn't live next door to each other anymore and we were too old for lemonade stands and we didn't take the same science class. And Joel was dead now. There was that, too.

"Where are you going? The school's that way." Madison motioned behind her. I could see how she was trying to smile, a little, at her joke, but not too much like it was funny. She was trying to be a good friend. But we both knew we weren't friends anymore. Not really.

"I'm going home," I said. It felt weird calling the new house "home." "I don't feel well."

Madison flicked the bottom of my braid, the way she used to when we were little. "Then you shouldn't walk. Can't your mom come get you?"

My mom. Interesting thought.

If I had pulled this kind of stunt back in junior high, my mom would've known I wasn't really sick. It would've been straight-back-to-school-young-lady, no questions asked. Unless she'd been having an off-day, of course.

Now she was always having an off-day. In fact, she probably wasn't even awake.

"She's busy," I told Madison, and started walking to show her I was serious. "It's okay, I like to walk." I did like to walk. Lame as it sounded, walking was my favorite kind of exercise. You could think things out while you walked. And when you walked, you actually went somewhere. You couldn't do that in volleyball.

"You shouldn't walk home alone, not if you're sick," said Madison, concern in her brown eyes. "I'll walk you home." She smiled again, and I knew the least I could do was accept this gesture.

"It's pretty far, to walk," I said, nodding my head east. Knob Farms was one of the Haven developments built on a terraced mountain—all uphill from the high school.

Madison looked up. You could barely make out the houses in my neighborhood from where we stood. "Too bad you don't have a car."

"Wouldn't matter if I did. I can't drive." I started walking faster.

"Yeah, but you'll learn," said Madison comfortingly,

putting her arm around my shoulder and giving me a little squeeze.

It bugged me, how her tone was so sure. As though she was telling a six-year-old that sure, she'll learn to ride without training wheels.

"No I won't," I said. It sounded way more wenchy than I'd intended it to. "Joel was teaching me to drive."

Madison hung her head—seriously, dropped it and looked at the ground, like an illustration for the description of "hanging one's head."

My heart beat faster with guilt. Bringing up Joel felt like cheating, somehow. I could see him shaking his head at me, saying, "Claire, don't use me to hurt people's feelings."

I wasn't sure what to say to take it back, though. And I didn't feel entirely sorry. Joel *was* teaching me to drive. His being dead didn't change that. Joel was the only one who could teach me, and he wasn't here anymore.

So Madison and I just walked for a very long minute. But it was only a minute, because I counted the seconds and got up to sixty when Madison said: "Well, I guess you could move someplace where you don't have to drive."

And without even thinking, I smiled. Same old Madison, same old problem solver. After all, if you can't drive and you can't learn, what else is left?

Madison smiled back, a huge smile with lots of

teeth. Madison hated to smile so widely that people could see her crooked back teeth, but sometimes she did on accident, and covered her mouth afterward.

Thing was, when she covered her mouth this time it bent some loose wire inside me. Madison didn't like other people to see her crooked teeth—but it used to be that I didn't count as "other people."

"So listen," Madison said, stepping around a divot in the cement. She was wearing flip-flops. I couldn't wear flip-flops because I always walked out of them. My toes wouldn't hold on to them right or something. I was wearing excruciatingly hot sneakers. Today was a piece of autumn. Why was it still perfect flip-flop weather? "There's something I've been wanting to ask you."

"Yeah?" I asked. Now that Madison had covered her teeth, I was hyper-aware of my sweaty-armpit marks. Had she already seen them? If I kept my arms down, would I be safe?

"Well, I wanted to know the whole story about K.L. Murray. I've only heard bits and pieces, and you know how everything gets messed up when you hear news after it's gone through, like, fifty other people."

"Kale Murray?" We had grown kale each summer in our garden before we moved to Knob Farms and our neighbors thought it was just another weird thing about the Espens, growing *kale* in their garden. It was just one more thing that made us stand out. I hated standing out like that, but it was like the rest of the family didn't even notice. Joel would always take the extra vegetables we grew to widows or new mothers in the ward, whoever he thought needed help. Superman mode again. As if kale could help anyone.

"Don't act all innocent!" Madison squealed. "It's all over school. I mean, he's like the hottest guy in the senior class, and he drew a picture of you! And he keeps it in his notebook! I know something's up with you two. Guys like K.L. Murray don't draw pictures of random sophomore girls."

"Wait . . . K.L. Murray's a person?"

Madison rolled her eyes. "Yeah, you know the super rich football player who just happens to live in your new neighborhood?" She grinned, walking on her toes like a ballerina at the beach.

"Well, obviously I don't," I said, walking faster, not caring if Madison couldn't keep up in her cutesy pink flip-flops. Why would I know this guy just because he was a hot rich football player who lived in my neighborhood? Lots of hot rich football players lived in my neighborhood. That's why it sucked.

It was like she didn't know me at all. Which she didn't. It's what made her bead six.

"So, you're not going to tell me what's going on?" Madison stuck out her lower lip. "Me, your best friend?"

I sighed. Here I was with a dead brother and a family that took the "fun" out of "dysfunctional," plus a two-living-room house in a town I couldn't stand. And Madison was girl-talking me about some football player who had some drawing in his notebook? It was probably a stick figure of his girlfriend, which Madison had interpreted as the stick-skinny Claire Espen. "We aren't best friends," I said. "You know that."

Madison jerked like I'd put an ice cube down her shirt. It was one of those things you didn't say, what I had just said. It was one of those things you whispered behind your ex-friend's back or wrote in a break-up note. You didn't just say it.

But I didn't care. I was sick of the rules here. I was done playing by them.

"I just remembered I have an English test I can't miss," Madison said. "Can you make it the rest of the way by yourself?" She didn't wait for me to say anything back. She spun around on her pink-foam-padded heels and took off.

Finally. I didn't realize I had been holding my breath until I sighed deep. K.L. Murray. The name didn't sound familiar. Maybe he was in on the conspiracy with Tate and Tucker. Maybe it was all part of their master plan, making me finally break the last connection I had to my former life—my friendship with Madison. Joke was on them, though. The friendship wasn't that great to start with.

Used to be it didn't matter who my friends were or weren't. Used to be my big sister Tabs and my big brother Joel were all I needed. I hung out with them. People called us The Three Musketeers, which I thought was cool until I got old enough to realize they didn't always mean it as a compliment. Okay, so some people thought it was weird, siblings being best friends. But I grew up thinking that was the way life worked: friends weren't that important, really, because they were temporary. Family was forever.

For as long as I could remember, we'd had a plaque in the front room with *Families Are Forever* stenciled on it in bold black letters. Every Monday night when we met for family home evening, I could see that plaque resting on the mantle.

Family home evening was a church thing. On Monday nights, nobody was allowed to go out or have other people over. We had to finish up our homework before Dad got home. Then we spent the evening together as a family. We started with a prayer, sang a song, read a scripture, and discussed family business (Tabs: "Could Claire please stop borrowing my clothes without asking?" Claire: "Can I please get more lunch money?" Joel: "I just want you all to know how much I love you. Group hug!").

Then we had a lesson, something about loving our neighbor, maybe, or the importance of tithing. Then we'd play a game—usually Scrabble if Tabs won out, Clue if I got to choose, and Uno if it was up to Joel. It was up to Joel a lot—he loved Uno. Mom always made treats for family home evening, and we'd end with family prayer, and it was lame but it also wasn't. It was safe and happy and predictable.

I always knew what to expect from Monday nights, back when we had family home evening.

In the new house, our plaque is nowhere to be seen.

Joel was dead. Dad was away at work. Mom was zoned out. Tabs had gone crazy and come back beautiful. Now she was just gone again, being a college student who "lived at home" in name only. My family was kaput. On the rosary of my worries, the other beads dimmed in comparison to that one.

Maybe families are forever, but I needed one right now.

I expected that the house would be quiet when I got home, but not as quiet as it actually was when I got there. I could hear things like the hum of the refrigerator and the tick of the clock in the hallway, things I had always thought people talked about hearing in books or on TV but never really heard.

The quiet house must have been what made me quiet, because my steps were soft down the hallway to Mom's room. Most kids who skipped school after spending approximately an hour there probably wouldn't make looking for their mother A-1 on the priority list. I wanted to be most kids, but I wasn't, so I opened her door.

She was asleep, so far under the rust-and-cream-colored duvet cover that I couldn't see her head. Hidden by a down comforter at ten o'clock on a ninety-degree Friday morning. Not good.

Maybe Mom had the right idea though, I thought as I closed her door and padded the opposite direction to my room. A nap sounded nice. No rosary of worries. No Goldens, no Madison, no driver's ed car. Nothing but sleep.

I could hardly keep my eyes open. I lay down.

The phone never rang at my house anymore. Dad had a Blackberry, Tabs had a cell, and Mom had no motivation to answer. So at first, through my haze of sleep, I thought the ringing was my alarm clock.

I hit what I thought was the snooze button but actually turned the radio on. I didn't use the clock's radio and it was set to some Latino station playing salsa music and static. Loudly. So I opened my eyes and was fumbling with the radio when I heard it again. Ringing. It was the phone.

I grabbed my black cordless and cradled it under my chin, yawning. "Hello?"

"Hi, Claire?"

"Uh, yeah?" I said, yawning again. I hoped the girl on the other end of the phone couldn't hear me. I checked the clock: 1:40. School got out early on Fridays, but still, classes had only ended twenty minutes ago. Nobody was asleep twenty minutes after school got out. Unless they'd skipped. What if this girl was a T.A. from the attendance office, calling to ream me out about my truancy? "Who is this?"

"It's Heather. Heather Hilton? I don't know if you know me. I live in Knob Farms, too. In the 1st Ward."

People in Haven described where they lived by telling you which Mormon congregation they were a part of. Like, instead of saying "I live down the street from Brad," they'd say, "I'm in the same ward as Brad." It had always creeped me out.

And it didn't explain why this girl was calling me. "Oh, okay. Hi." I was pretty sure I'd been in the deepest stage of sleep because all I wanted to do now was lie down.

"Yeah, well, I know you probably already have plans tonight and you totally don't have to come, but we just got this new projector and wired our basement for surround sound. So a bunch of us are going to watch *Too Many Goodbyes* and get pizza and stuff and it'd be great if you could come, too."

What? None of what she'd said made sense, but I couldn't figure out what to ask her besides: "Is *Too Many Goodbyes* even on DVD yet?"

"Nope," said Heather, sounding proud. "It doesn't technically come out for two weeks. But my dad just got back from a business trip to New York. He bought a bootleg copy in Chinatown."

"Oh. And you wanted me to come watch it with you because..."

"Only if you have time," she interrupted. "I mean, I know you and K.L. are probably doing something else tonight, after the game."

What was it with this K.L. person? Why was he ruining what was left of my life? Yawning again, I said: "Yeah. I think there's some party we're supposed to go to. I'll check though, okay? We'll swing by if we have a minute." Lying was kind of fun.

"Ooh, that'd be awesome," Heather squealed. "Do you need directions?"

"Nah, I think K.L. knows where you live," I said. "I'm pretty sure I've heard him mention you before."

"Yeah?" Heather was ecstatic but trying to hide it. Wasn't working. "Okay, then. Hope to see you guys there!"

"Sure." I turned the phone off. Hopefully I'd done some kind of life-altering damage. Hopefully I'd caused a major upset in the whole game that was the Haven High social scene.

I stretched my arms above my head and brought them down to my sides. Making up that whole alterna-life with K.L. Murray, Football God, had quenched my sleep craving. I looked at the clock again: 1:44.

Since I'd skipped school, I didn't have any home-work to do. I was way ahead in my classes anyway, because I actually studied in school and did my homework on time. I was even getting an A in driver's ed—on paper, I could drive.

The weekend had just emptied itself onto me and I didn't even have homework left to fill it up. I wasn't going to hang out with K.L. and I wasn't going to hang out with Heather. I wasn't going to hang out with Madison.

Last year at this time, Joel and Tabs and I would have gone mini-golfing before the West Haven Golf Course closed for the season. Or Joel and I would have helped Tabs study for her SATs. The three of us would have done something together.

Mom always said I was too dependent on Joel and Tabs. I think that's why she started sending me away, to Camp Westbrook in upstate New York. I'd gone every summer since I was eleven. Every summer except this last one. Joel died two days before I was supposed to leave.

I think Mom wanted to send me anyway, last summer, so she didn't have to deal with me. She loved having me at camp. When I came home, she'd always tell me my counselors raved about me and she'd say what a good traveler I was, to go clear across the country on my own. As if four summers at Westbrook made me some jet-setter.

Mom said I was more "competent" on my own. She said I did better without them.

I wish she'd never said that. Because now I was

without them, only I wasn't doing better. I was on my own, but I hadn't gone anywhere—they had.

Meanwhile, I was stuck in Haven. Totally stuck: I couldn't even drive.

Mom didn't have the right idea. Not about me doing better without my family. Not about her sleeping her life instead of living it.

Closing my eyes, I saw Madison, curling her brown ponytail around one finger, saying: "Well, I guess you could move some place where you don't have to drive."

It was the afternoon of the day I decided to leave.

......

URBANWORLD

The forum devoted to answering all your questions about city living!

Sept. 14, 01:52 PM

IDClaire   **Best U.S. Cities For A Non-Driver?**
Hi, I was just wondering the best city to live in as someone who doesn't drive? Thanks!

Sept. 14, 01:58 PM

rgw57   Lots of options: San Francisco
Philly
Boston
New York

Depends on where you want to live, though and where you can get a job.

CitEEBoy   i'd lean toward seattle or portland out west—cali (esp. sf) is getting too expensive! same with nyc, tho it's a great city!

IDClaire   Money and jobs aren't really an issue— I'm a student. And I am a little bit familiar with NY already. Never been to NYC, tho. Good public transportation, from what I see on TV. Is it good for walking?

CitEEBoy   R U independently wealthy, IDClaire? ha ha good name. R U going to Dclaire your independence and move to NY?

Eddy   NYC is a walker's paradise!

rgw57   I lived in NYC fifteen years and walked all the time. Subway is convenient,

though, and cabs are easy to get. Plus,
food and arts in NYC are tops.

SEPT. 14, 02:11 PM

IDClaire   Thanks, everyone. CitEEBoy, lol it's what
my brother called me. I guess in a way
I am going to DClaire my independence. NYC sounds like the place.

SEPT. 14, 02:12 PM

CitEEBoy   good luck!!!

....

My Move To New York

Phase 1: The Prep

- Order plane ticket—one way

- Make hotel reservations

- Arrange "ground transportation" from airport to
hotel

- Pack light and SENSIBLY—lots of layers; coat/
jacket; good walking shoes.

- Leave a note in case someone notices my
absence—long shot, but still. I'm at Madison's
for the weekend.

- Find online map of NYC/print it out

- Check cash supply. Necessary to "borrow" some
from Dad's top drawer?

In New York, autumn felt like autumn, not like a summer poser. It was the first thing I noticed after stepping off the airport tram that morning. There was wind: a brisk, skin-pricking wind I hadn't felt in so long. A wind I loved.

I adjusted the strap of my red Land's End carry-on so that it wasn't digging quite so deeply into my collarbone and checked the schedule posted on the board next to the railroad tracks. The next train to Manhattan didn't leave for another seven minutes—I could totally justify sitting down to wait for it. I had packed my squat, square bag with clothes on the inside, liquids and gels in the outside pocket, specifically so it would make a comfy impromptu chair.

The one thing I knew how to do was travel.

In fact, so far, making this trip had been easier than living my life at home. I'd made online arrangements, for a non-stop red-eye to Newark, with the credit card my parents had given me "for traveling" when I left for Westbrook one time. Now I used it all the time, ordering dinner or paying for school expenses.

I'd called an airport shuttle service to pick me up. I'd slept on the plane because airplanes put me to sleep, even ones whose passengers include an annoying high school orchestra from a school even deeper in Nowhere than Haven.

I was *so* finished with high school orchestras.

The other people were waiting for the train in a

glassed-in area, but the walls may as well have been cement given how little they looked at me. No one would notice me scouring a map, making sure I knew where I was going.

I'd gotten a hotel within easy walking distance of Penn Station, but I wanted to memorize the directions before I got off the train. No way was I going to look like a tourist, not even for a second. I may not have actually had a place to live yet, but this was definitely my new home.

New Yorkers were my people. They took trains. They sat in glass rooms but didn't watch you. Get off at 7th Avenue, take a right, take a left. Finding my way was that simple.

The train showed up almost a minute early according to my Timex, which I took as the first bead on my rosary of good omens. Even though the train car I entered was pretty full and I was planning to stand, a voice said, "this seat's empty."

It was from a woman with burgundy hair, a black felt hat, and lots of wrinkles. "Thanks." Bead number two.

Bead three was my bag sliding under the seat in front of me, a perfect fit, while the woman asked me where I was headed. Her smile made her wrinkles more prominent.

I liked how she asked that, even though I was obviously headed to New York. The only other stop was downtown Newark, and who heads to downtown Newark?

But she didn't ask me where I'd come from, and that was why I liked her.

"The city," I answered. "Do you work there?"

It was just like all those summers at Westbrook. I'd fly into Albany and squeeze into the maroon Westbrook van and every year I'd sit next to some girl who just needed me to ask one question, and in return she'd talk for forty-five minutes.

I watched the woman talk about the commute from Jersey, the ice skaters at Rockefeller Center, and seeing *Wicked* with her boyfriend, but every once in a while I let my gaze wander to the city skyline, until we went through a tunnel and after that the city wasn't a skyline anymore because I was in it. I said goodbye to the burgundy-haired woman, exited at 7th Avenue, took a right, took a left, found my hotel tucked between Broadway theaters, checked my bags, and looked for a place to sit down.

Moving is exhausting.

I stopped at a bakery and sat at a large communal table, where people were sipping coffee with cream and nibbling pain au chocolats, reading the *New York Times*. I shook my legs, to get out the I've-been-on-my-feet-so-long-it-hurts-to-be-off-them feeling. Hard to believe people here were just starting their day.

I ordered two perfect French rolls served with apricot jam, and Belgian cocoa—steaming frothed milk in a white ceramic mug without handles, with a smooth silver pitcher of thick dark chocolate.

I could definitely get used to this.

Phase 2: The House Hunt

- Option #1: Hudson Street between Chambers and Canal.

    It's so quiet around here—must be because it's a no honking zone (I ♥ no honking zones!). Tribeca isn't quiet the way Haven is quiet—hushed with silent judgment. This is the calm of a million different people doing a million different things without bugging anyone else.

- Option #2: Triangle between 6th Avenue, West Broadway, and Spring Street.

    I sit in a corner park here and watch a man and a little boy play street hockey outside a brownstone. The boy is wearing shin guards and when he hits the orange puck it spins in cyclones. The man—Dad?—never misses.

- Option #3: Broadway and West 8th Street.

    Something about this place just feels right.

By the time the sun was turning the city the golden-brown of chocolate chip cookies just before they burn, I was back at the hotel, beyond exhausted. My room was on the thirty-seventh floor.

Compared to the other hotel rooms I'd stayed in, including the dive in Cincinnati the airline had put me up in when they cancelled my connecting flight to

Albany one time, this room was small. Small, but it had everything—more than everything—I needed. Desk in the corner, flat-screen TV, puffy double bed. I ordered a seventeen-dollar cheeseburger from room service, soaked in the garden tub, then put on my blue, pink, and white plaid pajamas—the only ones I'd brought.

I came out of the bathroom and pulled the door closed. Directly in front of me was a decent-sized closet. The doors were mirrored, probably in an attempt to make the room seem bigger. It wasn't on purpose that I did it: stood in front of the mirror and looked deep into it. But once I did, it didn't take long to see Joel standing next to me.

I knew I wasn't imagining him, because he appeared fully-formed, with details I didn't remember until there he was, wearing that red-and-white-striped turtleneck everybody said made him look like the guy from those old *Where's Waldo?* books. He had freckles on his forehead—I'd thought that, like me, he just had freckles across his nose.

"Don't try to talk me out of this," I said, unbuttoning the top button of my pajamas. The steam from my bath must have been escaping under the door. The room was too hot.

"You know it won't solve anything," he said, getting that annoying parental tone he got all the time when he was alive. "Running away never solves anything."

"I'm not running away," I told him, moving closer

to the mirror, talking softer, noticing the sunburn spreading across my cheeks and nose. "I'm moving."

"Same thing."

"Mom and Dad moved us to Haven," I said back, too quickly. "No one told *them* they were running away."

"You don't have a choice about what they do." He said it calmly enough, evenly enough, for me to hate him. "Just about what *you* do."

"Shut up," I said, staring away from my reflection into his mirror-face. "Just shut up! Stop talking like you know everything! You always do that. You always think you know how to save everybody."

When I looked away from him I could see my face, stung with red from the tears or from the burn or from the anger or from all of it. "You couldn't save yourself, could you?" I took a breath. "Or at least, you didn't."

I backed up toward the bathroom door and slid down until I was a puddle on the floor, staring at Joel's New Balances. "You don't know what you're talking about. And you left me without a family. So it's too late for either of us."

"It is not," he said, in his stupid rah-rah peppy tone. "It's not."

"Yes it is." Pounding the glass next to his feet, I felt the warmth from his body. I could smell him. "You're dead. You're here right now, but when I need you, you're dead. Tabs is moving on and away from me, not that I blame her. Mom's comatose. I don't remember what

Dad looks like. I have to get away from them. I can't go on watching everything fall apart. I can't focus on making stupid U-turns when everything's falling apart!"

"Stand up, Claire," Joel said, and his voice was real—not all Superman, not all *I-can-fix-this*. He couldn't fix this. I knew he knew it, and I knew he knew I knew it, and he sounded so sad I almost couldn't bear it, I loved him so much again.

So I stood.

I stood, and I looked at him, and he was crying.

"I deClaire," he said, and tried to smile.

I tried to smile, too, but I was looking at him, not me, and I was pretty sure the smile wasn't much of one.

"I know this is hard for you." His tears were coming faster, but he wasn't crying harder. I could hear every word he said. "I know it is. But come on, Claire. Do you think it's easy for *me*?"

I reached out to touch him but the glass was cold and smooth, and I knew he wasn't there anymore, even before his image faded away.

The hotel had the most comfortable pillows my head had ever rested on, but I still didn't get much sleep.

So that morning I went to the place that felt right: Broadway and West 8th Street, an easy subway ride from my hotel.

How I've lived my whole life without knowing the clean efficiency of a subway, I don't know.

Greenwich Village was sun-drenched and glowing, and even this early on a Sunday morning people were out, enjoying what was probably one of autumn's last warm-windy weekends. Everything I saw made me happy. The night before felt distant, like a horror movie happening to a different girl, and the world was extra gorgeous to help sweep the flashbacks from my mind.

I stared up at narrow brownstones, marveled at wrought-iron gates, browsed through independent bookstores and ran my finger down the spine of Oscar Wilde biographies. Light danced over the man and woman, each with their head shaved, ranting about the president. Light swelled under the sign in the window announcing an anniversary celebration for Rafael and Justin.

I checked it closer. The party had been held the night before at a club, the name of which was printed in rainbow-colored letters. There was a picture of Rafael and Justin with their arms draped around each other, framed in a heart.

Wow.

No wonder this place felt right. I walked out onto the street and crossed at the corner, unsure of where I was wandering. It was a place where a man could throw an anniversary party with another man and still fit.

That's what I noticed about the glass—that you wouldn't think it would fit, but it did. At a table in front of me, an artist was selling colored-glass jewelry unlike any I'd ever seen before. Beads of raspberry-jam red were next to teardrops of cilantro green and eggplant purple, colors that even I wouldn't put next to each other. But the jewelry looked right. And as I knew it would, the ring I bought fit.

I fit. I fit in easy, no game-playing required. I pictured myself fitting into the townhouse above me, one that overlooked a park so small I wondered if it was actually a park, not a well-landscaped median.

It had to be a park. Medians didn't have statues, and this place did: two of them, all white, my favorite kind of statue. Crossing the street to get closer, I noticed that the park was paved in red brick and shaded with trees—elms, maybe? There was my beloved wrought-iron all around it. A haven.

A Haven that didn't suck. Finally.

I sat on a bench and looked at the statue couples. It took me way too long to notice they were gay.

The thing was, they looked sad, a little, but sure. Sure of what, though? Sure that they were different? Sure of how hard their love was going to be? Sure that they couldn't change it, even if they wanted to?

My heart sunk the way it always did when a memory I didn't want to remember was pushing its way into my brain. Unlike the memory you jog on purpose, this came with no warning and no reason.

It was Tabs who had told me we'd lost Joel. I don't know where Mom and Dad were. But she was the one to call me home from Madison's. The one who was always quiet. The crazy one.

I didn't want to come home. I needed to stay at Madison's. We had been talking about Promotion, the dance that welcomes incoming sophomores to Haven High and the first in a series of "orientation activities."

Unlike "Club Rush" and "Say No To Stress," this orientation activity was actually a big deal. Which was why we were discussing it ten weeks in advance.

"It's not like a real date," Madison was saying. "But Brayden and I are going to meet up there, and McKenzie and Josh, and Kaylee isn't sure yet who she'll be with at the time, but you know it will end up being Taylor Bransfield. But Claire, what about you?"

I could tell what was coming. She had asked me a question, but not direct enough for me to answer, not yet.

"The thing is, we'll all be there with guys, and we'll all have gone shopping that day, and you? You don't even care about that."

It was true. I wouldn't go shopping with them. I wouldn't spend the month of July convincing some guy to be my pseudo-date. I'd be at camp, and besides, I wasn't into that. But I was still into having friends. I wasn't into getting dumped by my only friends for some Promotion dance.

"You could always go with Joel," she said. She didn't say it mean, but it was mean, and we both knew it.

It was mean because Joel had taken Tabs to her

senior prom and everybody was talking about it. Moms thought it was cute but kids thought it was weird. Kids said Tabs was too crazy to get a real date, and that Joel had to be gay to give up a real prom night for a date with his sister. I knew Madison had heard, but I didn't know she was one of the ones laughing at them—at *us*.

"No," I said. "I won't. I'll—" I'd do something.

The phone rang. Madison ran to the hall to answer. She didn't have her own phone. Not many people in West Haven did. She brought the cordless into her room.

"Yeah, she's here." I could tell Madison was talking to Tabs because of how stiff her voice was. I wished it wasn't stiff. I wished Madison was better than I was, that she could be natural around Tabs. That she wouldn't think my family was crazy, me included.

"You need to come home," Tabs said, flat-voiced. It wasn't a clue, not in those days. Her voice was always flat.

"I can't," I said. I couldn't. Not unless I wanted to mess things up with Madison for good.

"You have to. Something happened to Joel."

Joel. On the camping trip. Great. Joel probably broke his leg trying to get someone's hat out of a bush or something. Why did he always have to be like that? Why did he always have to be Superman? Why couldn't he just have let Tabs sit out the prom? Why did he always have to try to fix everything?

"When's he getting home?" I asked, trying to get a few more minutes with Madison. I could convince her I wasn't like my family. I could get a guy. I could buy nail polish and body glitter. I could prove to her I wasn't weird.

"He's not getting home, Claire! He died!" Tabs' voice had gone from straight and even to hysterical. That's what crazy people did, right? They went from non-emotional to mega-emotional in a moment, making up stories that were only true to themselves. I was getting scared for Tabs, but I just rolled my eyes at Madison, like, *it's Tabs, what can I do?*

"He ran out of water, the rest of the troop is okay, I think, but he ... you've got to get home."

Now something in Tabs' voice sounded like the old Tabs. "I'll get home," I said. "I'm on my way." Looking at Madison, I saw her vacant eyes and the yawn she didn't cover up. I saw how in that one moment she stopped mattering.

The memory hurt like getting nicked with an old razor. I'd been over it so many times that the pain should have dulled. But it didn't. It hurt as much as it did when it was sharp, just in a different way.

The memory was the moment that set all the changes into motion—but for me it was the moment that everything stayed the same. Because Joel died, Mom and Dad got worse, we moved, Tabs got better. Everything changed except me. I was the one thing that stayed the same with Joel gone.

I was still the weird girl, the girl with her brother

and sister for best friends, the girl who didn't fit into Haven or West Haven, either. The girl who didn't fit anywhere. I tucked my hair behind my ear and twisted my ring. Had I liked not fitting? Had I liked staying the way I was when Joel was alive?

Joel was gone now. Maybe now, it was time to fit. Not just in New York, but everywhere.

And Joel's voice shook my brain, saying, "I know this is hard for you. But do you think it's easy for *me*?" and all the memories stung like razor burn and the Village started to spin. Like a million U-turns in a row, the Village started to spin.

Friday's child is loving and giving.

SEPTEMBER 26–28

NORAH

Joel
You called me Brunhilda,
The Peruvian Temptress
(You were the only one who did)
It's sinking in so slow
(That you're gone)

Miles doesn't care whether he graduates from high school or not. "Don't worry about it, Norah," he says. "It's under control."

Right. Under control. I slide fresh snickerdoodles onto a cooling rack. "You've got to go to school!"

"Lay off, little sis." Miles gets up from the kitchen table and in one swift motion swipes a cookie while knocking his Coke can into the garbage. "I'm shooting hoops with the guys. See you later." The cookie's got to be hot still, but of course it's not too hot for him. Not for Miles McGuire.

"We recycle!" I remind him.

But he's already gone.

I put my last sheet of cookies in the oven and get hit with a blast of hot air. It stings my eyes; makes them burn and tear up.

It would be so easy to cry now.

Instead, I set the timer and yell into the living room: "Who wants cookies? Just out of the oven!"

Everyone in this house looks like my mother—big eyes so dark they're almost black, long lashes, coarse brown-black hair. But I'm the only one with hair that poofs out every morning and skin so white my Peruvian mother couldn't believe I was actually hers. I guess I look more like my dad, but I really don't remember what he looks like. Not that I want to.

My dad's been gone so long that the memories I have with him in them are dark. Like they happened in another lifetime, when everything was black and hazy. But in my real lifetime, I've had a single mom. I've shared a room with my younger sister Ariane. And for the last year, my older sister Sandra and two daughters have been living with us too.

Ours is now a house of women.

Mom says it's hard to be the lone male. That's part of the reason Miles is "acting out."

But the bigger part is because Joel died. Everybody knows that; no one has to say it. Our family accepts that Miles can't handle the loss.

I'm unloading the dishwasher when Mom comes home from work. "Norita, my baby," she says, like a prayer. She sits at the kitchen table with her massive purse at her feet. Nanuk, Ariane's white bichon frise, starts yelping, pawing at Mom's legs. "How are the things on our home front?" My mom's accent is most pronounced when she's tired.

"The school called," I say. "Miles isn't going to graduate, Mom." I shake the water off a not-quite-dry plastic tumbler. "Can't you talk to them? Talk to *him*? Work something out?"

Mom sighs. She won't talk to the school. She hates stuff like that, and besides, her English isn't great.

And she won't talk to Miles. He usually tries to be gone when she's home, and when she catches up with him she's usually too tired for a confrontation.

It's so frustrating. "Mom, we have to do something about Miles," I say, softer, gentler, letting her know we're in this together. "You know we do."

Mom looks at me with her sad eyes. "You don't know what he's going through," she says. "You have to be patient with him."

I take a deep breath through my nose, because my jaw's clamped tight.

"Think about how you would feel if someone you were so close to died in such a tragedy."

I bite down on my tongue.

"You don't know what he's going through," she says again.

Why did she have to say it twice?

My Abuelita is not long for this world.

After dinner I take her some snickerdoodles, though I can't remember whether or not she's allowed to eat them. Abuelita has been in a nursing home on Sycamore since she fell and broke her hip two years ago. She's been sliding downhill ever since.

When I come to her door Abuelita senses me, because her eyes open into two slits. She mumbles something inaudible in Spanish.

Abuelita never learned English.

I take the chair next to her hospital bed and stroke her hand. Her veins stretch like lightning bolts, a bold blue against the paleness of her skin. Someone has given her a pink lily. Who? Mom and I are the only ones who see her, and Mom isn't the flowers type. The lily sits, unwilted, in a ceramic vase.

"Pretty flower," I say, and point. I don't know much Spanish. My mom speaks it, of course, but she never really taught it to us. Her only child who can actually converse in the language is Miles. Miles can learn anything just by hearing it spoken or seeing it done. He never has to study anything, which is how he got through twelve years of school with zero work.

Abuelita nods with her head still on the pillow. I don't know if she understood me or not. She doesn't say anything.

I shake up her snow globe of Minneapolis that one of the aides brought her. I hold it out and watch the flakes fizzle. "How are you, Abuelita?"

She coughs. *"Me gusta..."* Her words, so simple, come slow and unsteady.

"Yes?" I'm already reaching for the clear plastic cup of water on her bedside table.

"*Me gusta*... Miles. Me gusta Miles Anthony." She looks up at me with her sad eyes. *"Por favor?"*

Telling Miles that Abuelita needs him is going to be a waste of time.

I mean, I've already told Miles that *we* need him, and what good has that done?

Still, when he stumbles in from streetball, dripping sweat, I say to him: "Abuelita was asking about you tonight."

Miles goes straight to the fridge, doesn't say anything.

"She wants to see you," I say. "You should go."

For a split second I think maybe he will. For a split second his eyes go liquid and he's my brother again, not some lazy delinquent I don't recognize.

Then he slams the fridge door, holding a Coke in one hand. He gives a salute with the other. "Aye-aye, Cap'n. I'll go this weekend, okay?"

And I know he won't.

Miles glances at me and shakes his head. I'm rocking Sandra's baby, Adalia. "Pushover," he says, walking away from me.

Maybe I know that I'm a pushover. Maybe I know that Sandra should be rocking her daughter to sleep herself. But Sandra's been upstairs crying about something I can't decipher since I got back from Abuelita's, so it's me or nobody. Besides, it's easy for him to call me names when he's going upstairs to take a forty-five minute shower in the tub I cleaned, and dry himself off with the towel I washed.

If I wasn't a pushover, I'd never hear the end of it.

Miles says that I have a Cinderella complex. That I think if I scrub enough toilets and make enough loaves of banana bread, then Prince Charming will ride up on his big white horse and carry me off to his castle. (I hate it when Miles, Mr. Genius, mixes metaphors. I mean, as if Cinderella even *saw* a toilet.) I don't have a complex; I just like to feel needed. I'm not waiting for Prince Charming, either. I already found my prince charming, but nobody else knows it.

Not even Joel.

(I Hate You Because)
Now
I cry when I read Tolkien
Hear jazz on public radio
Change the station
Look away
When I pass
A Monet print
In the stationery
Department.
I hate that
Even in Walgreen's Five-and-Dime
You're still somehow
On my mind.

I wake to train songs.

I fall asleep to their low tones and I rise with their shrill whistles and steady moans. I like to hear trains thumping past me. Train songs sound like going home.

We've lived in West Haven, in a condo complex near the train tracks, for years now. Everybody else is used to the trains. They complained at first, but now they just sleep through them.

But I never take the train songs for granted. They're what lure me into and out of sleep. The train songs let me know that everything's going to be okay. Without them I would feel lonely.

The trains come early, about six. Gracie, Sandra's older daughter, is the easiest one to wake, so I start with her. "Hey Bunny, time to get up." She is snuggled on the loveseat she uses as a bed, golden curls splayed around her face like a mane. In this house of women, she is the only one with golden hair and crystal blue eyes, the genes of a fairy-tale princess. "Want some Cheerios?"

Her eyes flash open and she nods. Gracie is one of the few preschoolers still impressed by Cheerios. She pounds into the kitchen, and the sound makes Sandra stir in her bed on the couch. "What time is it?" she asks, falling back to sleep before I can give an answer.

While I'm getting the milk out my mom comes down the stairs. She leaves for work early because she commutes into the city. This morning, like every other morning, she looks tired. I've already got water boiling for herb tea. Lemon Zinger. It will help.

"Norita." Mom kisses my forehead. "My baby." She helps Gracie get her Winnie-the-Pooh bowl from the cupboard. "Cosita." She kisses Gracie. "Good morning."

Time to get Ariane, who likes to sleep late. "The water's ready, Mom." I head back upstairs. I've already put away my trundle, so I shake the daybed. Ariane has been known to sleep eleven hours straight, no small feat in a house with a five-year-old, a newborn, and a night owl who likes Nirvana. "Get up!"

"Can't," she says. "Headache."

It's nearly impossible to deal with Ariane when she gets like this. Even if she does get up, I'll have no way to make sure she gets to school. West Haven Junior High doesn't start until I've already been in class for a half hour. I knock on Miles' door for a solid thirty seconds, but it's equally useless.

Back in the kitchen, I open the fridge and take out the lunch I made last night. I grab a cereal bar from the kitchen and kiss Gracie goodbye. "Be good," I tell her, because her mother will forget to. Gracie promises she will. On my way out the door I tell Sandra it's seven thirty. This barely registers a grunt, so I'm off to school. Maybe Miles will show up after lunch, but let's be real. Looks like I'm flying solo at Haven High today.

We used to walk to school together, the four of us.

High school started out awesome. Every morning Joel and Tabs would come past our house on the way to school. Sometimes I'd make cinnamon rolls, the big, gooey kind, so we'd walk to school holding piping-hot pastries and getting frosting all over our faces.

Sometimes Joel and Miles would get lost in some sports conversation, so Tabs and I would fall behind and talk girl stuff. People say Tabs went crazy that year, but I never saw it coming. To me she was just this smart, serious girl who was really pretty but didn't wear make-up or the right clothes, so you couldn't tell unless you got up close. Sincere.

Once she asked me what was up with my dad. Did we ever see him? Did he ever write to us? Could I even remember him? I said no, no, and no.

"You can't remember *anything* about him?" Tabs looked at me, disbelief plastered on her face.

"Nope." I was uncomfortable talking about my dad, even in front of Tabs.

"You must remember something."

"Not really." Even before my dad left, he was always gone. I didn't have many firsthand memories of him, just a lot of secondhand stories from everybody else. Those secondhand stories made me hate him enough. I didn't need to add my memories to the mix.

"Just think a minute." I wished she'd leave me alone, but she was looking at me, waiting. "What do you remember?"

"My dad took me to the Greek Festival," I said. I have always been able to remember with clarity the things that I wish had never happened. "In the city. He made me eat squid. I begged him not to make me eat it. I cried and cried. But he made me eat it anyway." It seemed like a stupid, pathetic memory.

But Tabs looked almost pleased. "So you do remember something," she said with this sad, small smile.

After that, she stopped asking about my dad.

Later that year, when Tabs had her mental health issue and Miles' attendance started to drop to "sporadic," Joel and I would walk together, just the two of us.

I loved that. We'd talk about when we were kids. Not big stuff. Just little things, like that I wore my Care Bear T-shirt for a year straight when I was four, or that he had an obsession with unicycles that started the first time he went to the circus. He called me Brunhilda, the Peruvian Temptress. I laughed. (Brunhilda? That's not even a Peruvian name. A nickname like that was so *Joel*.)

Sometimes he would brush my hand with his (I never knew if it was an accident or not), and everything felt as close to perfect as my life could ever be.

Now, four months later, I walk to school alone.

At lunch I usually sit under the maple tree on the outskirts of campus, where I eat my peanut-butter-and-honey sandwich and write poetry. I'm not good at poetry, but I wish I was, so I write it and hope that eventually

I'll get better. Eventually, I'll stop thinking about Joel and that will get better, too. Eventually. I hope.

But today is too hot to eat outside. It's been hot each day since school started, but today I can actually feel my sandwich melting. On my way back into the cafeteria, I feel someone tug on my jacket. Claire. Joel's sister, a sophomore. I don't know her that well.

She is standing with a cluster of guys in letterman jackets and girls in student government sweaters. I never pegged Claire for the preppie-soc type, but since her family moved to Haven after Joel died, I haven't seen her at all.

"Hey Claire," I say.

"We were just going to get something to eat. You should come with us." Claire rubs the charm on her necklace, then smiles at me like she's asking a favor.

"Um ... that'd be great, I guess." For whatever reason, Claire wants me along, and I don't want to say no to her. I'm a Good Girl. I don't refuse invitations.

But I can't think of anything less great than eating with the Haven High elite, who are watching me now with mild curiosity only because they don't yet know I'm from the wrong side of the tracks.

"Awesome!" She smiles, more at everyone else than at me. "Guys, this is my friend Norah."

Friend?

They all nod "hello" and push through the double doors. Haven High's parking lot is divided into zones:

the S zone for faculty and staff, the A zone (closest to the building) for those with the expensive parking permits, and the B, C, and D zones. The D zone is so far from campus that you practically need a shuttle to get to the front doors.

Guess where Claire's new buddies are parked?

"Hop in," says a redheaded guy, clicking the keyless entry to a bright red Jetta. "I'm Trent, by the way."

I nod hello and am going to open the car door when somebody beats me to it. Someone with wavy golden hair and crystal blue eyes—the genes of a fairy-tale prince. "I'm Jonathan."

"Hi," I say. "And thanks." I slide in and glance over at Claire, who looks at me like "aren't you glad you came now?"

Claire's necklace is really a ring on a chain. I've never actually seen anyone wear a ring on a chain around her neck before. This doesn't look like the type of ring you'd wear around your neck, either—not like a promise ring or something. "I like your ring," I say, mostly out of curiosity. "Where did you get it?"

"New York." Claire's fingers fly to her chest again at the mention of her ring. Her thumb traces the loop, starting at the top, ending up where it started. "It changed me."

I'm not sure if she means New York or the ring, but something definitely changed her. She's not the same as she was when Joel was alive. Then again, who is?

"So, Norah," says Trent, "you a sophomore, too?" As he drives out of the lot, clusters of students part before him. He is Moses, guiding the Chosen People.

"Junior," I say, glancing at Jonathan.

"Just like us," Trent says. "I wonder why I haven't seen you around."

Trent's cell starts ringing in the tune of some annoying pop song. "Yeah? ... I don't care, just a sec." He turns to us. "Where do you wanna go for lunch?"

I shrug instead of saying, "isn't it customary *not* to look behind you while driving forward?" Claire shrugs, too.

"Alberto's?" Jonathan suggests. It's a deli in Haven next to the spa. I've never been.

Trent says into the phone, "How about Alberto's? Cool. Okay."

"You haven't lived until you've tried Alberto's albacore and avocado on sourdough," says Jonathan.

I think about the peanut-butter-and-honey sandwich in my backpack.

Alberto's is crazy busy.

I scan the menu up front, trying to see what's the cheapest.

Another huge wave of people sweep in, and it's the domino effect. Jonathan bumps up against me. "So, what'cha getting?" he asks.

I shrug. I can't stop doing that. "Don't know yet."

"Do you always talk this much?" He grins at me, a smile of white, even, perfect teeth. They're Haven teeth and they should bug me, but they don't.

Joel had a small gap between his front teeth—not a David Letterman gap, but a cute, slight-imperfection gap. Sometimes I'd imagine kissing him, and running my tongue through that narrow little gap.

When I look back on it, I can't believe I ever thought something so stupid, and I wish it had been a long time ago like when I was seven or eight.

But it was just last year.

We get up to the counter and Jonathan says, "Two albacore avocado on sourdough."

"Want to make them combo meals?" the girl behind the counter asks.

"Sure," says Jonathan, pulling a twenty out of his leather wallet.

I reach inside my pocket. At last count I had four dollars and eighty-three cents.

"No, I've got it," Jonathan says, touching my wrist. It's too intimate. But I like it.

"You don't have to do that," I say, though I have no idea if my $4.83 is going to cover it.

"I want to," he says.

"Your number's 682," the girl says, handing Jonathan a receipt.

"Over here guys!" Claire calls. They've taken over all the tables in the back section of the restaurant.

"Looks like we're being summoned," says Jonathan, and he smiles again.

Today, like most days, I go directly to the West Haven Library after school. I can't study at home—someone always needs something. And I like getting good grades. Good grades are something I have complete control over. I study for a bio test, outline a paper on *Dante's Inferno* for World Lit, and go over some French vocab.

Homework, check. Next stop: chaos.

When I get home from the library, Sandra is playing with Gracie while Adalia's napping. That's good—it's good to see Sandra up doing something.

"Hi Bunny," I say as Gracie races toward me.

"Hihihi!" Gracie squeals.

"Any luck with the job search?" I ask Sandra, to remind her she's looking for one.

"No one's hiring," Sandra says.

I go into the kitchen and take my peanut-butter-and-honey sandwich out of my backpack and open the fridge. Funny, no one's been hiring the whole time Sandra has been here.

But at least, here, Gracie and Adalia are looked after, even if I'm the one looking after them most of the time. I do wish Sandra would get a job, though, something to help get her out of bed in the morning. The women in my family have a history of choosing the wrong men.

Abuelita chose a much older man who liked the bottle. Sandra chose a man who liked to work even less than she does. My mom chose a man who liked other women.

I chose my brother's best friend—a guy who might have liked me or might not have, but didn't stick around long enough for me to find out either way.

I'm pouring myself a glass of grape juice when the phone rings.

It's Claire. "I know someone who likes you!"

"Claire?" I ask, just to double-check. I carry the phone into the half-bath off the kitchen and lock the door. Claire's never called me before. I barely even know Claire. Why is she expecting us to get all chummy?

"Duh! Of course. It's Jonathan."

"I thought you said it was Claire," I say, and smile at my reflection in the bathroom mirror. Zing.

"Ha ha," says Claire. "I mean it's Jonathan who likes you."

"And you figured this how?"

"Because he told me. He said he wanted to double with Trent and me on Friday night, and he asked if I would set him up with you. What do you say?"

What *do* I say? This is totally weird. The little sister of the guy who was my almost-boyfriend is trying to set me up with some Haven prepster with a leather wallet. But weird as it is, I want to do it. I think about Jonathan, with his blond hair and his nice teeth, and I think of him taking me somewhere special: I think about Friday night at the movies, dinner some place nice, a real date. I've never been on a real date before. I think about Friday night at home, playing with Gracie, or watching *Steel Magnolias* with Ariane and Nanuk, or rubbing my mother's swollen feet.

I want the date. I'm a sixteen-year-old girl, and I want the date. Someone likes me. Someone wants to take me on a date.

But Joel. What about Joel?

"I gotta check. I'll call you back," I tell her, and hang up the phone.

I Mean This In The Kindest Possible Way (But)
You took me with you when you left
I can't forgive you for that
(While I'm still here)

"So what's for dinner?" asks Sandra, coming into the kitchen.

She asks me that almost every night, and in her defense, sometimes she even helps. But tonight I'm just annoyed. "I haven't thought about it yet," I say.

"No need to get all crabby about it," Sandra says. "I was just asking."

She is wearing her slippers that make her look like she's wearing a big watermelon on each foot. Everybody in the house teases her about those slippers. She says they're like her security blanket.

"I'm sorry," I say. "I guess I'm just in a bad mood."

Usually Sandra gets the mail, in case Aaron, the ex, has "sent something." I don't know what she's expecting. Divorce papers? Child support? But the mail's almost always on the kitchen table when I get home.

Not today.

"Want me to go check the mail?" I bet Sandra didn't want to go out in her watermelon slippers.

"Yeah, thanks," she says, and smiles at me.

"Hey, Nanuk, want to take a little walk?" I ask, taking the leash from the closet. Our mailbox isn't in our front yard; it's joined together with about a dozen other mailboxes down the street. I grab the key.

Nanuk runs to my feet and starts panting when he hears his name. Poor dog—starved for attention. I haven't seen Ariane yet today, which means she probably hasn't walked him.

Our most faithful correspondents at this house are Discover, Capital One, and American Express, all of whom have sent something today. We also have so many ads that I almost don't see a thin white envelope nestled between an Old Navy circular and a coupon book for Rhodes roll dough.

It's addressed to me. In the corner, where the return address is supposed to be, there's only "Don McGuire." My father.

I open it outside, under the nearest streetlight. I don't want to open it at home—I could take it into the half-bath to read it by myself, but somebody would find it as soon as I came out, and the whole world would stop. Better to open it here, find out what he has to say. I hope he doesn't need money. Even if I did want to give him some, I don't have any.

His handwriting is still as bad as it always was. The letter is on a sheet of torn-out paper from a spiral notebook. It looks like a fourth grader wrote it.

Dear Norah,
I know this must be coming out of the blue and you haven't heard from me in a long time. Just know I think about you, my good, sweet girl. Please forgive me.

Don

Don.

He has not signed the letter "Dad." He has not even signed it "your father."

So I've got in my hand a letter from Don and the leash to somebody else's dog, who's yelping and tugging me toward our house.

I'm not ready to go back. Not yet.

"Sit," I say. I'm mad that no one ever taught Nanuk any patience, that no one in this family ever taught anyone anything. I yank on his leash.

He starts yelping again, but it's a softer, more pathetic

and less annoying yelp. Nanuk's white fur is matted and gray. He's been neglected. It's not his fault. I reach down and stroke his back, trying to fluff up the fur.

I'm a girl who is kind to animals. I'm a good, sweet girl, on her way home to make her family dinner. Who is picking up the mail for her sister. Who is trying to get her brother to graduate and her mother to stop looking around with those sad eyes. I am a good, sweet girl, who visits her grandmother who doesn't know her name or even want her around. I am a good, sweet girl whose father thinks will forgive him.

But truly, deep down, I'm not such a good, sweet girl. I'm a girl who's sick of making dinner. I'm a girl who will not forgive her father. I'm a girl with secrets.

It is starting to rain.

I walk into our house. I take Nanuk off his leash. I wash my hands. I start water boiling. I take out the spaghetti. I find the Haven High directory and I look up Claire's number. I dial the phone and say to her, "I'm in."

The Epitome of Innocence
If you ever ask me when
I loved you
(I don't think you will)
I'd say:
Back when you were easier to love.
Because:
When a girl in a ball gown loses a shoe

I applaud every time
That she finds it.
But:
When the boy with the orange breath loses his heart
I'm never the same
Once he finds it.

It isn't hard for me to remember that night. Because of course I've always been able to remember, with clarity, the things I wish never happened.

Miles was out with Lissa. Sandra and my mom and Ariane were out seeing *Too Many Goodbyes*, the year's blockbuster romantic comedy. Even though the movie had come out months ago, Mom waited to see it at Dollar Towne Theatres. It was so like my family to be seeing, in May, a movie everybody else saw over Christmas vacation.

Gracie had fallen asleep in front of the TV in my mom's room, and Adalia had been sleeping upstairs in her bassinet for hours. I was doing my homework like a good girl even though it was Friday night, because an empty house was a rarity and I wasn't about to let it slip away, even if it meant missing out on a three-and-a-half star movie.

It was raining that night, too. The showers had been coming in May, not April. I listened to the rain tapping on the glass and the ceiling. Perfect background music for a night of *Huck Finn* and laundry.

There was a knock at the door. I looked out the peephole and it was Joel, dripping wet, on the front porch. I let him in, even though I knew he wasn't there to see me. I was just someone for Joel to walk to school with. Miles was his real friend.

"Miles isn't here," I said. "He's out with Lissa."

"Big surprise." Joel smiled. His T-shirt was wet and clinging to his chest. Joel worked out for water polo, and it showed. I looked away.

"What'cha doing?" he asked, coming into the dining room. All my books were laid out on the kitchen table.

"Homework," I said, but I was mumbling it, nervous. I tried to see him without actually looking at him so he wouldn't think I was staring. The rain had changed him. It turned his hair the color of wet sand. It made his eyes greener. Wet, his red shirt looked burgundy. I folded my arms across my chest. "You know me. I'm always doing homework"

Joel laughed. "I do know you. And I still don't get how you and Miles can be related." He picked up *Huck Finn*. "I read this last year. Do you have Everett?"

My mouth was dry. It hadn't been, until Joel showed up. "Yeah. I do."

"So did I. She wasn't bad." He took the book over to the couch and settled in. "I liked this," he said, trying to find one of the passages. "What about you?" He looked at me with those clear green eyes.

"We ... we just started it," I said, watching him. He knew Miles wasn't home. He knew Miles wouldn't be home anytime soon. He was staying anyway.

"So where is everybody?" Joel asked.

"A movie," I said, sitting on the arm of the recliner. "The one at Dollar Towne."

"That chick flick?" he asked, and I nodded.

"And you didn't want to see it?"

"I couldn't pass up an empty house."

He laughed again. "Yeah, in this house that's a rarity."

"Exactly." I was too warm. I was wanting him to stay but thinking maybe he should leave. My whole body was throbbing. I was thinking how he was a guy and I was a girl and how maybe he should leave.

Joel looked up from *Huck Finn*. "There's something I want to show you," he said. "Come here a sec, will you?"

"Okay." I tried to sit as far away from him as I could and still see the book. I didn't want him to hear my heart beating or see the longing jump out of my body.

A good girl would never feel this way about a boy. Who was in her house. With nobody else around. But I was feeling that way, and it was feeling so good.

And he moved closer to me. At least I thought he did. I don't know just how it happened but all of a sudden we were sitting closer than we had been. Close enough that I could smell his breath. He had been eating a Starburst or Skittles or some kind of orange candy before he came in, because that was what he smelled like. Orange.

And he looked me in the eyes and I saw green, green, green, spearmint-toothpaste-gel green and that was all, and he gulped, his Adam's apple bobbing and it was so cute, and he said, "Norah, I have a crush on you," and then he put his mouth on my mouth and he kissed me. It felt so good, like a kiss is supposed to feel—I knew it even though I had never kissed anybody else. It felt so soft and warm and smelled like orange and Joel, and he put his hand over my hand.

We both pulled away from each other at the same time and I said, "You're all wet still." And I dared to put out my hand and touch his shirt, and run my fingers over his chest. "Your shirt, too, it's dripping wet."

We kissed again, another baby kiss, a short, sweet kiss, and then another, and then we kissed a real kiss. A real kiss because we both wanted it and we both knew we both wanted it, so we didn't need to stop—we just kept going.

"Oh, Brunhilda," he said, running his fingers through my hair, "my Peruvian Temptress." And he kissed my neck and I giggled, because it tickled and I was so glad he had called me his Peruvian Temptress, because that's what I wanted to be. I wanted to tempt him and I wanted him to tempt me and I didn't want us to be Good Girl and Nice Guy, I wanted us to be together and feel things, like what we were feeling now.

I didn't care about everything we had learned in seminary or at church or at youth camp. We kissed longer and I didn't care that I wasn't supposed to be alone on a couch with a boy and he wasn't supposed to kiss a girl for longer than three seconds. I cared about now, because it was so good and so right and it was Joel, Joel who I had wanted for so long, with so much of myself. It was everything coming true, finally, and I was feeling his shirt still and the muscles underneath, wishing they were closer to me, so I moved closer.

He moved closer, too, and he was touching my neck and my shoulders and running his fingers along the scoop neckline of my T-shirt. "Your shirt is still wet," I said. "I could put it in the dryer for you. I'm doing laundry. I'm always doing laundry."

Joel didn't laugh. He said "Better take it off first," and he smiled, but only a hint of a smile.

So I did. I reached down to the hem of the shirt and pulled it off him and threw it to the floor. His chest was smooth and knotted with muscles. And then he was reaching down and pulling off my shirt. I was thinking *wait, wait*, but more of me was thinking *hurry, hurry*.

I didn't want him to see my flat chest, my little bra with the teeny white bow in the middle, but I was amazed that he wanted to see it. He took off my shirt and threw it down on the floor next to his and put his arms around me and held me. I looked into his eyes and smiled, but he didn't smile back, and he didn't look happy, and his eyes weren't green, green, green—they were darker and sadder, and his eyebrows were all crinkled up.

And he let go of me.

He let go of me and grabbed his shirt off the floor and put it back on, inside out.

"I'm sorry, Norah," he said. "I'm so, so sorry. Please forgive me." And he took about three steps and he was out the front door, the rain still pounding down.

And I just stood there in my jeans and my little bra with the teeny white bow in the middle, and watched him go even long after he was gone.

Then I put on my T-shirt with the scoop neckline, stacked up all my books, put the last load of clothes in the dryer, turned out the lights, locked up, and cried myself to sleep.

On Friday night, I decide to borrow something of Ariane's for my date. She's the fashion plate in the house. And the beauty. Since she and I share a closet, it won't be too hard to find something that's just the right amount of trendy.

Usually when she comes home from shopping with Mom, with bags and bags of clothes (none of them for Mom), I feel a ball of anger burning low in my stomach. We can't afford all these clothes even if they are on sale, even if Ariane does look great in them, even if Mom is so old she doesn't need new clothes. But this time as I go to the closet, our ocean of debt isn't on my mind for once.

Jonathan is on my mind: his white, even teeth with no gaps, his smooth way of talking and laughing. Jonathan wouldn't make out with a girl and run away, apologizing and not looking her in the eye. He wouldn't ignore her for days after that, except to look at her in the halls sometimes, and mouth: "I'm sorry." He wouldn't leave on a trip to the Grand Canyon and then die, without even saying goodbye, without ever explaining what he meant by that night, and why he wished it never happened. Was it me? Was it something I did? Was he scared to be something besides Mr. Nice Guy? Scared to break the rules about what you were allowed to do with a girl? Jonathan would never leave me with these questions. Jonathan would be cool.

I borrow an outfit I won't feel self-conscious and poor in: a red fitted T-shirt with *Hollister* across the front (red is my best color), dark-rinse low-rise jeans that barely fit, and a corduroy jacket because it's been cold, lately, at night.

I comb my hair and add the expensive gel so it won't frizz up if it starts raining or gets ready to. I borrow Victoria's Secret body lotion from Sandra without asking her, either (I am not such a good girl).

"Pretty Bunny," says Gracie when she sees me. Gracie loves everybody in this house, but she has a special nickname only for me.

"Where are you going?" Sandra demands. She's holding Adalia and staring at nothing I can see.

"On a date," I say as calmly as I can, like I deserve it and it's also obvious. I should go on a date. Sixteen-year-old girls should get to go on dates. Sixteen-year-old girls shouldn't stay home on Friday night baking cookies and doing laundry. I wiggle my foot in my shoe, where I've stuck the folded-up letter from my father.

"No need to get defensive," says Sandra. "Have a good time," she adds.

Jonathan comes over then, ten minutes after he said he'd be there, at that perfect place between late and on time. "Trent and Claire are in the car," he says. "Are you ready to go?" He looks around like he's expecting to have to meet someone, do the whole yes-sir-home-by-twelve-nice-to-meet-you routine. But that's the thing about not having a dad. He's not around and Mom is too exhausted to care. Besides, she's visiting Abuelita.

"Yeah, let's go," I say.

Gracie says: "Where are you going?" because she's not used to me leaving at night.

"I'll be home soon," I say, and blow her a kiss. She blows one back, and I step out into the fresh air and close the door.

"Is that your sister?" asks Jonathan.

"Niece," I say. "Sister's daughter."

"Aah," he says, and puts his arm around me, natural as anything.

Why can't I be natural back? Why do my shoulders stiffen with his touch?

"Did you have trouble finding my house?" I ask, because our place is hidden in a mess of condos.

"Nope," he says, "your directions were just right."

Trent is driving his Jetta and Claire is up front, so Jonathan and I climb in back.

Nobody with money goes on dates in Haven, where Barnes & Noble is the only establishment open after nine p.m. We drive into the real city—Salt Lake—to a glitzy outdoor mall. We eat at a Brazilian restaurant, where they bring around platters of exotic food—hickory-roasted chicken hearts and grilled slabs of pineapple and salads with hard-boiled ostrich eggs.

Claire and Trent and Jonathan are laughing and joking with each other. Claire eats a piece of bacon-wrapped turkey breast off Trent's skewer. Joel's dead and she's still happy.

But he saw me with without a shirt on. Did he think I could forget that?

"What's wrong, Nor? Try a bite of something nasty?" Jonathan is smiling and holding out his napkin. "Go ahead, spit it out. I don't mind."

Claire and Trent laugh.

"Thanks," I say. "I'm okay."

There's no way I'm gonna spit it out. I can't. Besides, it wouldn't be fair to Joel.

We walk over to the megaplex and catch an action

movie of no interest to me. After a few minutes, Jonathan reaches over to hold my hand. His hand feels warm, but holding it doesn't make my hand tingle the way it did with Joel.

But Joel left me. Joel's gone. Gone without explaining; gone without saying goodbye. Joel's gone, and my father's gone, and no matter what I do my brother's leaving me, too. Miles can't handle the loss. But I have to.

So I lay my head on Jonathan's shoulder, because I can, because I'm not some good girl who doesn't do that.

Even when my neck gets sore, I don't move my head.

Saturday's child must work hard for a living.

LISSA

She worked part-time at Grampa Bob's Close-Out Super Store. Grampa Bob's bought up all the things the other stores didn't want anymore and sold them at a discount.

Actually, it was a pretty humiliating job.

On days when they got a big shipment of over-stocks like laundry detergent or frozen lasagna, Lissa had to dress up in overalls, a flannel shirt, and a straw hat, pretending to be Grampa Bob. Did it *matter* if it was a million degrees out? Did it *matter* that there was not, nor was there ever, a Grampa Bob? Did it *matter* that she was a girl?

She'd stand out on the corner of Dandelion and 1st to attract customers. She'd wave her arms around and wear a sandwich board that said, *Come see the Cream of the Crop!!!*

Miles always called Grampa Bob's the "cream of the crap," but Lissa never saw him complaining when she brought home extra bags of misshapen Jelly Bellies at the end of the day.

That day, in the first week of October, she was paint-ing the windows at Grampa Bob's. She was in charge of writing things like *Tide: 8.99 a bottle* or *Happy 4th of July!* Today's message read: *Too Many Good Buys!* a play on the title of the movie *Too Many Goodbyes* that had just been released on DVD. Kevin, the manager, liked to capitalize on other people's successes.

It was one of those Indian-summer afternoons when she thought the sun would stretch out forever, stretch out right over her without curling up to take a break. The window paint was getting soupy and crusty, both, from the heat.

It was when she turned away from the window (where the customers in line were staring at her) to wipe her forehead with the back of her hand that she saw him. He was standing at the bus stop on the other side of the Grampa Bob's parking lot.

Calling the row of parking spaces in front of Grampa Bob's a "parking lot" was an overstatement. Calling the bus sign the guy was standing under a "bus stop" was an overstatement, too. No bench there or anything. So, basically, he stood fully unobstructed only a few yards away. Basically, she had a clear view of him, him with his gray sweatpants and navy blue polo and goatee and dark green backpack. He lifted his wrist to check the time and then, like he could feel her looking at him, turned his head toward her.

She looked back into her window.

The scenario was a strange one. For one thing, the guy was not much older than her. But Lissa had lived in this town, in the very same house, her entire life and she had never seen him before. She could guarantee it.

Also, nobody who was a teenager in the Haven/ West Haven area took the bus. People who were too young to drive or didn't have a car looked for rides anywhere they could get them, or rode bikes or even walked. There was no place to go too far from where you already were, anyway.

And he was wearing sweats. In ninety-degree weather! In public! Without even the decency to be ashamed of it. Gray sweatpants? With a goatee? Lissa couldn't figure out what kind of a statement *that* was supposed to make—he couldn't pull off the beret-and-nightclub vibe wearing sweatpants, but he couldn't be Mr. Lives-in-Workout-Clothes while wearing a polo shirt. Plus the goatee was stupid. It looked ugly, as goatees almost always did.

But the strangest thing about the situation was this: the sight of his face took her breath away.

By the time she got off work, he was gone. Of course. He had been waiting for a bus. It probably picked him up and took him where he was going and he had probably been there for a long time by now. But her gaze still swept across the parking lot, checking.

Lissa drove a Plymouth that had lived in Haven even longer than she had. It was a hand-me-down from the seven brothers and sisters before her, all of whom drove it around in high school, grew up, and passed it on. The car was like a million yearbooks, none of them hers. It occurred to her, as she drove away and saw Kevin locking up, that Grampa Bob's was the only place in her whole, wide world that was really hers.

Her town had been founded by her fourth great-grandparents. Her house, the one she'd grown up in, was the same house her father grew up in, and his father before him. The basement bedroom she slept in used to be her sister Rachel's until she went away to BYU. Before that it was Andrew's. She couldn't remember whose it was before that.

Her school was full of secretaries who remembered her sisters, football coaches who asked after her brothers, and teachers on the verge of retirement who had taught her aunts and uncles. Her friends were the children of her parents' friends. And Miles. Even Miles wasn't really hers.

When people asked her why she worked at Grampa Bob's (after all, she was pretty and well-liked and hardly a Grampa Bob's kind of girl, if there were such a thing), Lissa would just smile and say, "Hey, it's a living."

But it was more than that. Grampa Bob's, with its no-name cola and animal crackers labeled in Mandarin, it was totally hers.

And the mystery man in sweats and a goatee—he was hers, too.

It surprised Lissa to see Miles waiting on her front porch when she got home. Usually she had to beg him to come over, or he'd call and say he'd be right over and then never show. But now Miles was on her front porch, not even rocking on the swing, just sitting on the step waiting. Miles never waited; never just sat there.

Lissa knew he wasn't waiting for her—not really. His gaze wasn't on her, it was on the house next door.

She wanted to tell him it hadn't changed since the last time he saw it. The *For Sale* sign was still planted firmly in the front yard, growing leaflets instead of leaves. On Saturday mornings, when she drove to work, Lissa saw Brother Jensen out mowing the lawn. He didn't have to do it. It wasn't his lawn. But everybody in the ward felt like they had to do something. Lissa wondered how long Brother Jensen would be mowing the old Espen lawn before somebody finally moved in.

The ward took it hard when Joel died. Lissa's mom was the Relief Society president, so she fielded questions and offers of help for days and days afterward. People were bringing the Espens breakfast, lunch, and dinner right up until they moved. Sister Carr, who was on the school board, got the district to set up the Joel E. Espen Memorial Scholarship. In church, members stood at the pulpit and related stories about Joel when they gave talks on service, or compassion, or charity. Everybody took it hard—but they all *did* something about it. That's how Mormons grieve—they do things.

But Miles. Miles took it hardest. And he wasn't doing anything about it. He wasn't doing anything at all.

"Hey," Lissa said tentatively, trying to gauge Miles'

mood. Angry? Melancholy? Lonely? She could never tell anymore. "What's up?"

"Norah is *so* harshing my mellow," Miles said.

Lissa could tell he was trying to be funny, trying to smile. "Yeah?"

"Yeah. *We need groceries. You're never home. Mom wants you to finish high school.* She's the one who wants me to finish high school, not Mom. She thinks she's all boss and making the world all great, but really she's just a huge pain in the ass. Now she's all over me to get a job."

Grampa Bob's wasn't so bad. Lissa could get him a job there, easy. But Miles wasn't interested. She knew; he told her that every time she dared bring it up.

Norah wanted Miles to be respectable: get over the slacker attitude, get over Joel's death, get a job, help out around the house, and be the model big brother to try and make up for their dad leaving. Irasema, Miles' mom, was way past hoping for that. So was Lissa. Norah was trying to save Miles, but Miles was way beyond saving. He'd been way beyond saving for a long time.

Lissa just said: "Your family could probably use the money," because they could.

"Liss," Miles said, touching her hair. "Just be pretty, okay?"

She knew he was trying to be funny again—trying to change the subject in some over-the-top, I'm-Miles-McGuire-and-can-get-by-on-my-charisma-alone way.

And maybe she would have thought it was funny, back before Joel died, back before Miles changed.

But now—now her scalp tensed up under the weight of his hand. "Want to stay for dinner?" she asked, even though he never did.

Miles wasn't on a meal schedule like a regular person. He woke up after most people ate lunch, then skipped breakfast and snacked on Coke and Doritos. At night he'd go with his friends to get nachos at Taco Bell or mooch free food if one of his groupies was working at Dairy Queen. Everyone was a sucker for the McGuire charm—or what was left of it, anyway.

Miles stood up, smiled, and looked Lissa right in the eyes. It struck her again how handsome he was; how lucky she was to be with him. Thick black hair, eyes deep-dark like a secret, and that *smile*.

"Yeah," he said, smiling still. "I want to stay for dinner."

He did? He *did?*

Miles put his arm around her and it was like old times, how his touch made her tingle with acceptance and anticipation. "What are we having?"

"Good news, Lissa," Kevin told her when he called the next day before her shift. "We just got a motherload from Kellogg's."

Good news for Kevin was always bad news for

Lissa. She traded in her lime-green tee for the flannel shirt and dreaded overalls.

She wasn't in the best of moods, anyway. Miles had been in a funk all last night. He barely said two words to her parents during dinner, and even though they had spaghetti, one of the few real foods he liked, with garlic bread and tossed salad and even sparkling cider to complete it, Miles didn't comment on the meal or even thank her mom, which Lissa knew burned her up inside.

Lissa's family knew about Miles. The whole ward knew about Miles, knew about his family's "situation."

On a map, the West Haven 11th Ward boundaries looked like a slice of pizza. Lissa's house and Joel's house were at the top, where the pizza crust bent into a frowny-face. At the bottom of the slice—the teensy-tip—were the condos, where Miles lived.

Sometimes people looked down on the condos. Not literally down because they were at the bottom of the pizza slice, but down because the people who lived there were usually as close to broke as people got in Haven.

She was the first girl to meet Miles when he moved into the ward, and it was a point of pride with her. She deserved him because she met him first.

Lissa and her dad always helped people move into the ward. Lissa was skinny but strong, and she liked bringing things into an empty house. All that space. And the people moving in could make it theirs however they wanted to. Since she'd never gotten to move, this felt like the next best thing.

One Saturday morning when she was in ninth grade, Lissa and her dad picked up a dozen Krispy Kremes and headed down to the condos.

Miles McGuire jumped out of a too-full pickup truck. Then he smiled at her, this amazing smile with these perfect lips.

"Got any glazed?" he asked.

She nodded, then remembered she could speak and said, "Shouldn't we actually *do* something first?"

He was still smiling as he opened the donut box and took two. He gave one to her and said, "We are doing something. We're eating."

Lissa's dad had gotten called to be the McGuires' home teacher, which meant that every month he visited their family. He'd share a gospel message and ask what he could do to help them out, and it turned out he could do a lot.

Miles' dad had just left them, his mom had a bunch of kids still at home and a part-time job, and everything was falling apart. So Lissa's parents stepped in: Dad got Irasema a job as a receptionist for a friend of a friend, and Mom sometimes ran errands for their family.

Once, Lissa's mom picked her up from school because she had a dentist appointment. Mom picked up Miles, too, because he had a group project at the West

Haven library and it was too cold to walk. It was humiliating, sitting in the front seat of the minivan, with him behind her. She just knew he was staring at her. She wasn't sure if it was a good thing or a bad thing.

Now Lissa's family was used to Miles' family—used to Miles himself. But last night had stretched the goodwill of even her sainted mother.

All Miles did was pick fights while he and Lissa were watching TV. "*The Real World* sucks," he said, changing the channel. "You're the only person in America who still likes this show." Miles was the one who liked *The Real World*, not her. He would make fun of the characters, yell at the screen. It could be fun, watching TV with him.

Lissa imagined she and Miles were on their own reality show, where they got sent to some swank house in a city five hundred miles away from Haven with five hundred times as many people in it. She wondered if it'd be different there, if Miles would really be hers, if they could get away from everything here that was dragging them down.

But it was more than this place that was dragging them down, she knew. They couldn't just leave the place behind and leave the problems. The problems could live in the *Real World* house, too. Norah. Irasema. Miles' dad—because if anyone could track him down, it would be MTV.

And Joel. Of course Joel would live in the house.

Lissa thought that maybe, even with all those people wandering around, she and Miles would still have a chance. That's what she wanted: for she and Miles to have a real shot at a real relationship.

Still, she couldn't help herself from adding one more roommate to the mix—one wearing gray sweats and a goatee.

They ended up watching celebrity poker, which she hated and Miles wasn't even paying attention to.

"Talk to me, Miles," Lissa said, leaning her head on his shoulder the way he liked her to. "What's really bothering you?"

"Shh," he said, pressing the volume *up* button on the remote control. "Just be pretty."

Lissa's head burned where it was touching his shoulder. She sucked in her breath and held it there.

She showed up for work in regulation hick attire, clocked in, and went into the bathroom to tuck her hair into a straw hat, which was tacky but kept the sun off her face.

"Don't forget your sandwich board," said Kevin from behind the register.

Like she could. She grabbed the sandwich board and walked straight out the door and onto the corner of Dandelion and 1st. And then ... then it was like it used to be with Miles, how time slowed down when she saw him, and how seeing him felt like a birthday present.

He was standing under that same bus sign. Still wearing the gray sweats (unless it was a different pair), with the goatee and the green backpack slung over his shoulder, which was so straight-out-of-the-eighties that she laughed louder than she intended—because his get-up was so strange, he was so stunning, and she wasn't paying attention to stuff like how loud her laugh was.

He heard her. The corner of Dandelion and 1st was not that big a corner.

He looked at her for a long time. "Something funny?"

"Your outfit," she said before she could stop herself. Part of her wanted to be embarrassed in front of him. Part of her wanted to say anything that would get a response from him, no matter what it was, just as long as he kept looking at her.

He arched an eyebrow. She loved guys with thick eyebrows, and his were the thickest. "*My* outfit?" he said, looking her up and down.

"You know I don't usually dress like this," she said, wondering why she added the *you know* part.

But he said, "Yeah, I know," like he wasn't even surprised. "Do you always work this shift?"

He wore a nice silver watch, one you wouldn't expect on a guy with (a) gray sweats or (b) a goatee. Just as he had yesterday, he lifted his wrist to check the time—a swift motion showing the curve of his neck. The guys Lissa knew didn't wear watches, never cared what time it was.

"On weeknights," she said.

He nodded. "What time do you get off?"

"At six." Her parents didn't like her working late on school nights.

"Then tomorrow night, I can see you?"

She'd have to come up with an excuse for meeting a guy on a school night. A guy her parents had never met. A guy *she'd* barely met. She'd have to go to a lot of trouble.

"At seven," she said.

Technically, she was with Miles.

Well, as much as anyone could really be with Miles.

Miles had never been the girlfriend type—more the girl*friends* type—so Lissa never thought she had a chance with him. Never dreamed she'd have a chance with him.

Not that she wasn't dreaming about him anyway. She was. During the day and during the night.

Sometimes, at church, he'd flirt with her. Or at least she thought it was flirting. But then he'd talk to other girls the same way, smiling that same smile, and she thought, *forget it.*

But it didn't take her too long to realize that Miles flirted with everybody. Not in a sexual way, like someone usually flirts. In a way that demanded attention, telling everyone he met: *Look at me. I'm funny and smart and handsome. Admit it—you like me.* Girl, guy, parent, child—people liked Miles. Often in spite of the fact that he was Miles.

Which was where Joel came in.

Lissa had thought, on more than one occasion, how in any other world, in any other universe, Miles and Joel would never have happened. That's what their friendship did: it happened, the way linoleum peels when it gets old, the way dust accumulates, the way frozen things melt. It just happened.

One Sunday started out the same way the Sunday before it had, with Miles getting ogled by a bunch of girls who were all wearing the same dress, just made out of different fabric. It was after Sunday School, before Sacrament Meeting, so everybody was standing around the foyer waiting.

Lissa looked up at the glass display case hanging on the far wall: the missionary wall. Everyone who left on a mission from the West Haven 11th Ward had a plaque hanging there until they got back. She read the plaques, looked at the pictures of the newly-called Elders with their clean faces and respectable haircuts. Most of those guys weren't much older than she was. Some of them were coming home soon. She could date one of them, but she wouldn't.

It wasn't that Lissa liked bad boys. Or that she didn't like nice guys. It was that she liked Miles.

The organ music started up, then, so people knew the meeting was about to start. On her way into the chapel, Lissa briefly scanned the area for Miles. And there he was, talking to Joel. Then he was laughing, smiling his smile at Joel; then he was sitting down on the pew next to Joel and his family, and those other girls were looking at each other, and Lissa could practically see the confusion floating above their heads put into words: *Joel Espen?*

Lissa never thought of herself as growing up next door to Joel so much as next door to the Espens. There were three Espen kids, all about her age, all outside her group of friends. At church, when all the young men and young women met together, most people sat by their friends. Not the Espen kids. They all sat together, laughing like they were in some club.

Not an exclusive club, though, because Joel was always inviting people into it. He remembered things like what classes people took or where they worked or what teams they played on, and would ask them about it and be all Good Samaritan. It was nice, but more strange.

That was Joel—Mr. Nice Guy, but the kid definitely marched to this drummer only he could hear.

Once Lissa's oldest brother, Darren, came back to the house just to chill and mooch food. Which would have been fine, except then he said: "What's that hot-shot McGuire kid doing playing basketball with Joel?"

It was a valid question, but she was still too hot with anger to answer it. Guys like Miles didn't have friends like Joel. But couldn't they if they wanted to?

Lissa would be lying if she said she didn't start hanging around outside her house more just to get Miles' attention. She thought for sure Joel would see right through her, but he was just so nice that he didn't, or he did but didn't care.

So she'd be out shooting hoops in her driveway and Joel and Miles would be shooting hoops next door. And Joel was Joel so he'd invite her over, and they'd talk, and Joel would bring out baby carrots and OJ—which was a lame-A Joel-snack, but whatever. It was Joel's house, anyway. And that was how it started, the three of them.

One night they were in Lissa's yard jumping on the tramp, celebrating it being warm and spring and not caring how lame-A it was to jump on a tramp when you were a junior in high school.

It was getting late, because the sun was setting, when Joel left. He wanted to finish reading the Book of Mormon before school got out, and he was almost done, but the year was almost over.

Miles was like, "Dude, that is so lame-A," which he always said because he couldn't swear around Joel. But

Miles smiled when he said it, which he always did, so Joel took off. It was just Miles and Lissa.

They stretched out on the tramp, arms crossed behind their heads, looking at clouds and waiting for stars. Lissa noticed how her hair fell around her like a blond waterfall, wondered if Miles noticed, too.

He turned over and stared at her. She could feel it, and it wasn't like those times in junior high. This time he stared *at* her, and she knew it was a good thing so she turned and stared back. He had chosen her. In a world where everyone she knew knew him, he had still chosen her.

She looked into his eyes, those deep-dark eyes, and saw those lips, and knew the reason he chose her was because she was her, and she knew he was going to kiss her and she was right, and at that moment, it became the two of them.

So, technically, she was with Miles.

To get ready for her date, Lissa pushed around in one of the drawers under her sink to find her bottle of vanilla oil, which still had a few drops left in it. She rubbed it between her breasts, put on a Better Than Ezra T-shirt and brushed her hair until it was shining. She didn't bother curling it. She wasn't sure why—it just seemed like this time she didn't need to.

She drove the Plymouth to the Grampa Bob's parking lot, parked, and walked over to the bus stop. She had three minutes to go before seven o'clock. She was prepared to wait, but then saw him strolling up to her: khaki shorts, trimmed goatee, and the green backpack with the straps on both shoulders. She sucked her breath in because *whoa*, he was gorgeous. "Hello," he said to her.

"Hello," she said to him back

"Where do you want to go?" he asked, and she said "Anywhere," and they started walking.

When Lissa first got together with Miles it was like she couldn't breathe around him, let alone hold a normal conversation. When they talked, they'd flirt. That was pretty much how she always was with guys. Laugh, joke, sure, but it was all so they'd like you, think you were cute, talk about you to their friends. Everyone knew that was how you talked to members of the opposite sex, even if they were just friends or whatever. It was always like, *be cool, be cool.*

But with the goatee guy, it wasn't all *be cool, be cool.* Not to say her heart wasn't beating a million miles a minute—it was—but not because she was thinking of a good comeback or wondering if she had food in her teeth.

She liked the way her footsteps matched his—how they walked in time to each other without even trying. "I think Oasis is the most underrated band ever," she said. It was totally random—had nothing to do with anything. But she said it anyway. "I think those people who say they're Beatles rip-offs are insane."

Miles had never heard of Oasis, and she played him stuff but he only pretended to listen. He thought she couldn't tell, but she could.

"Noel and Liam are gods," goatee guy said.

"Sometimes I imagine myself playing the guitar in the subway station, playing 'Wonderwall' and singing so my voice echoes off the station walls. And you know what? I don't even play the guitar."

"Or live near a subway," he pointed out.

"Yeah. Or live near a subway." She couldn't explain why she didn't feel stupid mentioning all of this. She should have been humiliated. There she was, walking down Dandelion with a total stranger, rambling about old pop songs. But instead she felt lighter than helium.

"There's an art exhibit in the basement of the library," he said. "Work by high school kids, but it should still be interesting."

"Yeah," she said, nodding. She'd go anywhere with him, but the art exhibit sounded cool. It was the kind of thing she could never drag Miles to even if he was comatose.

The Haven Library was this old, white-brick building that was ugly sixties-style old, not cute/quaint/charming old. People usually had piano recitals and town meetings in the basement, and Lissa had never been down there before. It was exactly right that her first time seeing it should be with him; that even in this town where she'd lived her entire life, he still had something new to show her.

She hadn't expected to see anything new at the art show, either, but almost everything she saw was interesting to her. Not bad-interesting or weird-interesting, but *interesting* interesting. As they looked at things, he didn't say much, which she loved—except at the exact right times, which she loved even more. Like when they passed by a painting of Beauty and the Beast and saw it was untitled. He said: "No title? Sure, why bother? It's Sleeping Beauty, obviously," and winked at her. Things like that.

There was a cool still-life by Lissa's friend Mandy, who she knew liked art but who she didn't know was an artist. It looked like one of the art classes had made papier-mâché masks—a few were on display. And there was a breathtaking landscape by Adlen Murray—a junior Lissa didn't know at all, but wow.

"Wow," he said, sucking in his breath, staring at the glistening shades of red, the cool ceramic blues, everything.

Lissa wanted to pull him against her, hard, and kiss him and not stop.

They wandered into another nook, a nook in shadow where she could kiss him if she dared, which of course she didn't. The nook was filled with collages—everywhere, distorted pictures were hanging, cut from whatever they used to be and made into this—into this beautiful *thing*. She thought it must be amazing to be part of something so small and simple, and then be made better, be made into artwork, just by being in the hands of someone so skilled.

It made her wish she had even an ounce of artistic ability.

He came up behind her as she stared at one, a picture that from far away looked like just one set of lips, but up close you could see was made up of hundreds of small pairs of magazine-picture lips. He rested his hands on her shoulders, and she tried to look at the lips without thinking about lips.

"You like this one?" he asked, and she nodded. She did.

"Me, too," he said. "I like how everything is just part of a part of a part."

Lissa nodded again. She was listening but she was also drifting above herself, so that she was not inside herself, she was watching from above. Watching *them* from above: his hands on her shoulders, his hands stroking her hair, his lips and her lips and all the lips taking over in this secluded nook, where she could kiss him if she dared.

"We should see what's in the other room," she said. It was like she wasn't really saying it, she was just watching herself say it, and from above she was irritated with the girl she saw. The girl should stay there; she should linger.

"Portraits, I think," was all he said, walking out of the nook into the bigger, open room with the back wall of windows. It was completely dark outside. Only a few orange lights glowed from the senior center.

The light glided her back inside her body and she took a deep, gasping breath. How long had it been since she breathed?

Some of the portraits were not that good—people seemed to have a particular problem with noses. Noses and lips. Lips again—she turned away.

When she saw it she realized she both expected to see it and didn't expect to see it. She wasn't planning to see it, but when she did, it didn't surprise her.

It was Joel, and it was just right. He had that not-light-but-not-dark hair parted on the left side, and it made him look young, so young, like he was when he died. His eyes shone bright, bright and glowing, even though the drawing was in black and white. And those freckles. Joel's freckles.

Lissa wasn't a crier. Her dad said she "took it in stride," which he was glad about. He was almost finished raising four girls when she came along. He said he was so old he wouldn't have been able to take the tears, so God blessed him with a girl who wouldn't give him any to deal with. She hadn't. She just wasn't a crier.

That was why she didn't know what to do when

tears started streaming down her face and her nose got drippy, and they were broken-finger tears or stepping-barefoot-on-a-rusty-nail tears—big tears that couldn't be held back.

He put his arm around her. "Why don't we get out of here?" he said, and she didn't even answer, she just followed him.

The library backed onto a park. They sat under a tree on a memorial bench for some guy on the city council who died of cancer at the young age of forty-nine. All Lissa could think was, *forty-nine is three times longer than Joel got to live.*

They sat there and he didn't say anything, or ask her if she was okay because she obviously wasn't. Miles wouldn't know how to handle her upset. When she was with Miles, she couldn't be upset. Only one of them could be high maintenance, and Miles had claimed that title long ago. Long before she even knew what she was getting into.

"How long is he going to punish me?" Lissa said in between sobs, surprising herself. She didn't intend to say it. She didn't intend to say anything at all. "How long is he going to make me pay because I haven't suffered the way he has?"

She hunched over because her nose was drippy and she didn't have a tissue. He couldn't see her with snot running down her face, so she tried to sniff it up while keeping some dignity. But she knew he didn't care about her nose or about her crying, either. He traced patterns into her back, softly.

"Who's punishing you?" he asked.

"Miles." She sniffed, wiped right above her lip with the back of her hand, and looked up. "He acts like I don't feel a loss, but I do. Every day I do." Miles lost Joel, but Lissa lost Miles.

"A loss?" He was still stroking her back.

Consciously, she knew it must be unbearable to lose a friendship like Joel and Miles had, one that came as natural as breathing. But inside, she felt that losing her relationship with Miles was worse—it was a relationship she had worked for, cultivated for so long. Losing Miles was harder than losing Joel. Miles was still alive.

But she couldn't tell this guy all that. So she said, "Joel. We lost Joel."

He crinkled his eyebrows, the way people do when they're watching the last three minutes of a really good mystery on TV. "Was that a drawing of him? That drawing we saw before we left?"

She nodded and sniffed again. "That drawing was exactly like Joel. *Exactly* like." She shivered. This day had been so hot. This night was so cold.

Because she shivered, or perhaps just because he wanted to, he put his arm around her. Instant warmth spread through her body.

Heat never felt good like this. Heat was anger. Heat

took and gave nothing in return. Heat never felt good like it did now.

The good heat made her heart beat faster. The good heat made her say it: "Joel loved Miles, too. I thought I loved Miles. I thought I was the only one who could love him so much—who could want him so desperately. Who could need him, you know?"

Lissa knew she was breaking every guy-rule she had ever learned, but it didn't matter. His arm was still around her, tighter than before.

"And when he chose me to be his girlfriend, it was like I had won something. A prize that's better than a prize because you've wanted it for so long. You get the prize, but you get the wanting, too. When you get it, you get everything."

She remembered nights playing ball, when she and Miles would toss the basketball between them, leaving Joel out. It was only for a few seconds, but Lissa remembered how Joel looked when it happened. *He's mine*, she told Joel on those nights, getting rotation on the ball, tossing it up above his head, straight into Miles' hands. *I get him. Not you.*

"You *thought* you loved Miles?"

Lissa knew what he was thinking. She hardly knew this guy, but she knew he didn't want to steal someone's girlfriend. "Thought," she said. "Past tense."

Joel loved Miles without any hope of Miles loving him in return. But Lissa's love was only fueled by the idea that if she worked hard enough, she could get him. It made it clearer which one was real.

She was cuddled in his arms now, breathing deep and steady. The heat made her say it: "Want to know the last thing he said to me?"

"The last thing who said to you?" he asked, and she realized that he hadn't been in her thoughts, knowing she was thinking about Joel. He didn't know anything about Joel. The memory of Joel didn't haunt their conversation, the way it did when she was talking to Miles.

"Joel," she said. "He came over to my house. We were next-door neighbors, so it shouldn't have been weird, but it was. He never came over without Miles. There were tears in his eyes. I knew why he had come over. I knew his heart was breaking. He said: 'He loves you, Melissa. Take care of him for me.' Then he left." Lissa sniffed, but she managed to control her voice. "I never saw him again."

"Melissa." He said it slow and beautiful. "Your name is Melissa."

"No one calls me Melissa," she said. "Only Joel called me Melissa."

"Can I call you Melissa?" he asked. He looked into her eyes and *whoa,* he was gorgeous.

She nodded. "What can I call you?"

"My name's Adam," he said. "Call me that."

"Adam," she said, and it sounded just right. "I don't

love Miles. I never loved Miles. I loved having Miles. Except I never really did."

But technically, she did have Miles. Technically, she needed to take care of Miles. She was no better than Norah, on a mission to save someone who didn't want saving. "I need to take care of Miles." The weight of saying it aloud made her stomach tighten. "Joel wants me to take care of Miles but I don't know how!"

Adam stroked her hand. "I don't want you to leave Miles, not if you don't think it's right. But I don't think Joel would have wanted you to stay with Miles. Miles needs to take care of himself. Joel knows that now."

"Do you really think so?" she looked up at Adam, because how could he know what Joel knew?

"Joel would want you to be happy." Adam smiled, and it was so warm her heart melted, gummi-bears-in-a-hot-car melted. "He was a nice guy, right?"

"Yeah," she said, "he was." Adam hadn't known Joel, didn't know Miles, wasn't part of their history. Right then, Adam was just hers. Wanted to be just hers.

"Want to get something to eat?" he said, and Lissa watched his beautiful lips forming the words. She saw them getting something to eat, talking until late. She saw him coming over the next morning to see her, her still in pajamas, neither of them caring. She saw them eating breakfast with her parents. She saw herself buttering toast and saying, "This is Adam. You don't know him yet, but you'll like him."

"I'm starving," she said as he helped her up. He had beautiful lips, and someday very soon she saw herself kissing them.

But not today.

Today, technically, she was with Miles.

Called to Serve
WEST HAVEN ELEVENTH WARD MISSIONARIES

Elder Shawn Allred
CHILE ANTOFAGASTA MISSION

Elder Chase Williams
WISCONSIN MILWAUKEE MISSION

Elder Ethan Smedley
BRAZIL SAO PAULO SOUTH MISSION

Sister Cathryn Knoles
CANADA CALGARY ALBERTA MISSION

Elder Jason Morgan
TAIWAN TAICHUNG MISSION

Elder Austin Richardson
CALIFORNIA OAKLAND MISSION

Sister Genevieve Morgan
ENGLAND BIRMINGHAM MISSION

Joel Espen
CALLED TO HIS HEAVENLY HOME

©2008 Brittany Lisonbee

About the Author

Even as a child, Emily Wing Smith had overly thick
eyebrows, a passion for writing, and a tendency toward
attending odd schools. So it wasn't much of a surprise
when she graduated first with a BA in English from
Brigham Young University, and later with an MFA in
Writing for Children from Vermont College. It's also
no real shocker that she spends too much money on
eyebrow waxing.

Emily lives with her husband in Salt Lake City,
where she writes, bakes chocolate chip cookies, and
occasionally substitutes at her old high school (which
hasn't gotten any less odd). This is her first novel. Visit
her online at www.emilywingsmith.com.

A Conversation with Emily Wing Smith

You've told this story through six different voices, but it's a book as much about who is missing as who is present—the "he" of the title is dead when the book begins, after all. What made you want to write a book in six voices about a seventh voice that was silenced? What were the challenges of writing six very different, and occasionally only loosely connected, characters and stories?

As a teenager, I moved to a community where a boy my age had recently died on a camping trip. Occasionally, I would meet people who had known and loved him, and I was amazed by their diversity—Bad Boys, Good Girls, and everyone in-between. It's interesting to get to know someone only through what others say about him—especially when you know you won't get the chance to meet him.

Different voices kept coming into my head, talking to me about how they were dealing with this tragedy—but none of the voices were from the boy himself. As the voices came to me, I would write down snatches of what they said (interestingly, very few of these "snatches" remain in the book). I would draw lines from one voice to another as their connections became clearer to me. As I figured out more about each character's role in Joel's life, and his role in theirs, I would draw more lines. It's actually a pretty inefficient way to write a book, and I wouldn't recommend it, but for me it was the only way.

Religion and sexuality play pivotal roles in your book, but not always in the ways one might expect. Characters aren't simply religious or not, and sexuality doesn't seem to be as simple as gay or straight. I've had many discussions with other readers about Joel and, while we all love the book, we don't necessarily agree on who Joel was—a dilemma we share with the characters in the book (I love how Tabbatha immediately challenges our assumptions about Joel on page 15). At the end, it's not a book with any easy conclusions (I suspect it's not a coincidence that it's a book filled with people who love debate). Talk a little bit about writing a book that takes on so many "hot-button" issues but avoids being preachy or didactic.

When I started this story, it had exactly zero plot.

I had a bunch of characters with very strong voices, a vague idea of their mutual friend, and that was it. Further complicating things was their mutual friend being dead. When I had the idea for the nursery rhyme, things started linking together. I never thought about it taking on "hot button issues."

The deeper I got into the story, the more natural certain questions became. Why would you give up something you knew you needed? How do you reconcile what you believe with what you feel? My hope is that readers will be able to reach their own answers to the questions the book raises.

Your book also very cleverly addresses the difficulty everyone has reconciling people and stories that defy common notions of what is normal, right, or possible. For example, when Tabbatha reads her work in class, the first response she gets is disbelief: "Impossible. I mean, just the logistics of it. There's no way your parents could move so quickly after their son died"—and yet the story is true. At the same time, though, Tabbatha has a very similar reaction to the notion that anyone in Haven could be gay, especially her brother, until she's confronted with it head on. Was it important to you that this be a book that asked more questions than it gave answers?

Early on in the writing process, *The Way He Lived* was critiqued in a workshop. Most people found it unbelievable—that someone could die in such a manner, that a family could move so quickly after such a tragedy, even that such a place as Haven could exist. True events were dismissed as impossible.

I continued writing. Instead of changing the story, however, I worked the group's criticism into it. We all make assumptions, whether or not we try to, and whether or not we vocalize them. I started thinking about the assumptions people would make about my characters and the assumptions they would make about others.

The setting of The Way He Lived *is an important part of the book. It's very particular and will be somewhat unfamiliar to most readers, but at the same time parts feel very universal—particularly the distinction between affluent Haven and less affluent West Haven. Tabbatha, who just moved from West Haven to Haven, says: "I'm staring into a city that isn't entirely normal, but from a place that is much stranger." Norah, from West Haven, refers to someone as having "Haven teeth." Talk a little about the role the setting plays in this book.*

I spent many years living in a city nearly identical to Haven/West Haven. I think moving there in high school made me hyper-aware of its quirks—instead of just figuring out a new school, I was also figuring out a new lifestyle.

Parts of it were so cliché—the big houses up on the hill and the smaller, older ones on the west side of the railroad tracks, for example. I think the struggle between the "haves" and the "have-nots" is universal. But in a lot of ways my city—and Haven/West Haven—is unique. The predominant religion shapes the culture, and that seems natural to those who live there. This story couldn't have taken place anywhere else.

Grief is central to your book but, once again, there's no one kind of grieving—sadness is not simple. Grief permeates the characters' lives in unavoidable and surprising ways, and the different kinds of pain they feel seem to reflect the different ways Joel touched their lives. I wonder how you see the distinctions and how you came to write them.

I thought a lot about the stages of grieving when writing this book—denial, anger, bargaining, depression, and, finally, acceptance. I thought about which character would be in which stage. Ultimately, I wanted to show how grief over the loss of Joel motivated them to change in some way—whether for better or worse, whether the change was permanent or temporary.

The young adult genre has gotten a lot of attention lately, and there's a lot of discussion about what makes a book "YA," as opposed to "adult." In your mind, what makes this book YA?

I didn't give any thought to whether or not my book would be young adult. I've wanted to write young adult fiction since the time I was a young adult myself. I read YA literature in junior high and high school, studied YA literature in college, and specialized in YA literature in graduate school. I feel the same way a lot of YA authors feel: that in my heart, I will forever be seventeen years old.

My own feelings aside, however, I think *The Way He Lived* is a young adult book because of its tone. While many books for adults feature young adult characters, adult books generally have the tone of "look at what I've learned." The tone in my book (and I think this is true of young adult books in general) is "learn with me."